CAN SHOWBIZZERS CRUSH CRIME?

CAN SHOWBIZZERS CRUSH CRIME?

A Max Royster Mystery

by Frank Hickey

Library of Congress
Catalogue-in-Publication Data

Can Showbizzers Crush Crime? / Frank Hickey
1. Fiction – Crime 2. Fiction – Mystery 3. Fiction – Hardboiled

Published by Pigtown Books, an imprint of
Hidden Pearl Books L.L.C.

ISBN: 978-0-9848810-5-5

For further information, please contact:

info@pigtownbooks.com

10 9 8 7 6 5 4 3 2 1

Second Edition / First Issue

To Jim Mowat, U.S. Merchant Marine,
(Retired), and all my other good friends
in the High Desert town of
Barstow, California

Prologue

New Yorkers did not get what they wanted this Christmas. I sure did not.

On the day after Christmas, I hobbled on a cane along Manhattan's 86th Street subway platform. The station smelled of garbage and illegal cigarette smoke. The cold clawed.

A Dad in winter tweeds and a loud attitude followed his Son through the turnstile. He was wide and starting to soften in the middle.

The Son skittered onto the platform and towards the front end. The train would come in there – it was where suicide jumpers went.

The Son looked like a vessel about to break up on the rocks. His fair skin flushed from emotion under an expensive haircut. His body was pouching into fat already. Dad would not like that.

Sixty feet away by the turnstiles, out of their sight, an NYPD cop leaned against the wall and kicked his shoes free of the slush that lay above us on the streets. He had a narrow foxy face, pale skin and two moles sprouting hair on his neck,

"I'm Royster," I said to the cop. "Off the Job. There's a father-son act on the platform. Getting out of hand. He might be a jumper."

"We can't do nothing until he jumps," the cop said. "You know that, being off the Job."

I blew out a breath and leaned on my cane. My doctor wanted to operate on my knee today.

"Did you ever hear of Preventive Patrol?" I asked.

"Did you ever fricking hear of minding your own goddamn business?" he asked.

"Civil servant," I said.

Then I limped back onto the platform and neared Dad and Son.

"Hey, hey," I shouted. "You guys need a referee?"

I was trying to be a regular guy, all bluff and hearty.

It never worked for me.

A subway noise got louder. The train was coming.

"No money," Dad said to me. "No spare change"

"I don't want money," I said. "What's going on here with you and Junior?"

"That's our business. Now leave us, please."

"Who the hell are you?"

"I used to be with the Police Department," I said.

The statement was the truth. But I mumbled the beginning of the sentence, stressing the words "Police Department."

New York law could not arrest you for saying that you were a cop if you were a civilian. You had to show or wear something that looked official to get arrested.

They could not arrest me for mumbling.

"Show me your badge or else go chase yourself," Dad said.

"That's right," the Son said.

Now they were united against me, the Common Enemy.

The train pulled in and stopped.

The danger passed.

We all got in the same car.

Dad glared at me until I left the train.

Chapter 1

I'll Follow the Sun

"I'm operating on Wednesday," the doctor said. "Then you'll be on crutches for about three months."

"I would rather sandpaper a monkey," I said. "January and two more months in Manhattan, hobbling around? Why so long?"

"Because you put off this operation," the doctor said through her lisp.

Dyed walnut hair fell over her tortoise-shell glasses. Her teeth gleamed, reminding me that she had munched sugar cane as a child.

"That always complicates an operation. And those kicks really mangled your knee."

"How about waiting until spring?"

"By that time, you may be much worse off. You've waited too long already."

"January here is ice-cold sleety windy hell," I said.

An idea hit me.

I swiveled around on the exam couch.

"Doctor Viega, how healthy am I, generally?"

"Overall, better than you deserve. You weigh too much at two-sixteen and six feet tall. Redheaded people are supposed to be hot-tempered and choleric, but your blood pressure is okay. Your family had eye problems. Do you have anything like glaucoma or retinal detachments?"

"This sounds silly, but I don't know how bad my eyes are," I said. "Perhaps I'm legally blind. The cops were too lazy to check when they swore me in. DMV let me squint at the chart. Just to be safe, I walk a lot and avoid driving as much as possible."

"How many times a week do you drink alcohol?"

"Sometimes not enough."

"A cigar smoker, too. You should be more active. Get out running around Central Park."

"I'm headed there now. I don't run. I just ferry my fat around and pray for a belly miracle. What I mean is, when can I travel after I undergo this knife of yours?"

"You can't. Traveling will be too painful."

"Wintering and stuck in my cubbyhole apartment will be more painful," I said. "So cut me Wednesday like you promised. And I'm fleeing this slush as soon as I come out of the ether."

Somehow, that is what I did.

೪

Friday morning, I rolled over in agony, trying to ignore my left knee bandage. I punched in Pat's number and waited for him to pick up.

"Y'hello?" Pat had crafted this New York combination of "Yeah" and "Hello" into one word.

"This TV reporter lady hit me up in Carlow's East Bar," he breathed. "She wanted to know about us Playpen Irregulars. How we help you handle cases just like Sherlock Holmes used his raggedy bunch of kids, the Baker Street Irregulars. She says that you must be a great motivator to get us knockaround guys like me to help you."

"Yeah, Pat, I'm a great motivator."

"You're ignoring me again."

"You still flying skiers down to Pennsylvania on the weekend?" I asked. "You got room for a broke-down ex-cop on crutches? I been putting off your seaplane ride offer too long."

"The mountain is really frozen this year," he said in his whiskey and tobacco morning voice. "You hate the cold weather."

"That's why I'm taking Amtrak west from there."

"Going where?"

"California."

☙

That afternoon, I fought slush with the tips of my crutches and dragged myself over snow crusts to York Avenue.

The cab brought me to the seaplane dock near Wall Street. My crutches clattered into the motorboat that ferried me out to Pat's seaplane.

The choppy East River tossed the seaplane on its pontoons. Waves lapped.

"You look dead" was Pat's greeting.

"This wind is cutting," I said. "Slush soaked my feet. They'll stay wet all night. Let's fly before the painkillers make me hurl again."

Pat looked like an aging leprechaun.

He sported blue eyes of an innocent babe. Reddish whiskey cheeks flowed down to a softening neck and hard round beer belly.

Four skiers slouched in the back.

Pat started singing "Come Fly with Me," copying Sinatra's style. The skiers stared.

"Ready?" he asked. Pagan joy lit up those eyes.

The plane's prop started spinning. Water skittered. I could feel myself grinning.

Singing with him, I watched the river water speed past us.

"Now, we're up!" I breathed. "California or bust!"

☙

We swooped down over icy-looking pine trees onto a lake where ice formed near the shore. The sky was colored like lead pencil shavings. White water crested up from our pontoons as we landed. More cold knifed down past my collarbones and shriveled me.

ᥱᥤ

The next day saw me headed west on Amtrak. My crutches nestled against the metal-rimmed seats.

Drugs kept me sleepy.

My fingers speared out my contact lenses so that I could sleep. The eyeglasses that I wore instead had lime-green colored frames with lenses shaped like hearts.

The train headed west under oyster-colored skies.

"Car accident?" a florid-faced man under a pure white crew-cut asked somewhere in Pennsylvania.

"Pretty near," I said. "Between the pain and the knock-out drugs, I'm trying not to think about it."

"Sorry."

That was Pennsylvania.

I ached to get West.

ᥱᥤ

Ohio formed an ice-storm that rattled and chilled the window. My cheek rested on the seat back near the glass.

"Going straight through to Los Angeles?" the conductor asked. He sported gold-rimmed eyeglasses and a brushy black moustache. Old acne scars pitted his cheeks. The hair around his temples was silvering and the moustache looked a bit too black. He probably dyed the moustache in order to preen for the passengers.

"I'll probably get off before then," I said. "Someplace warm and friendly, where I can crutch around without a rental car."

"Maybe Houston?"

"Bad memories in Houston."

ᥱᥤ

In Illinois, a golden-haired college-type young woman duffle-bagged her way on. She sat in front of me and drawled to different boyfriends on her cellphone. She stared at my glasses.

"My Lord, whatever happened to you?" she said.

"Do I look that bad?"

"Well, I don't mean bad. But those crutches and all. What happened?"

"The strength of a tiger is incredible," I said.

"What's that?"

"One of Ace Hume's best pick-up lines."

She regarded me.

"Have you been to the club car?" she asked. "The bar?"

"Not on crutches. You can't get there from here. I've been living on this jumbo bag of Mediterranean food of hummus, cracked-wheat crackers, feta cheese going bad, breadsticks, olives, halvah and dried sausage. I need the bottled water that they sell here in the car."

Her lipsticky mouth formed a moue.

"Now, if you don't want to talk about your foot," she said.

"Knee," I said. "A marker of my horrible past."

"How did you hurt your knee, then?"

"Fighting with a murderous sex deviate who was schooled in the killing arts –"

"Well," she said. "If you're going to make up stories."

When I woke up again, she had gone.

The wind howled outside.

It chilled my palm against the window.

"Make up stories," I muttered, trying to copy her drawl.

The train kept lulling me to sleep.

❧

My cellphone buzzed.

"Max, this is Jody," a womanly voice said on the phone. "How have you been? We haven't talked in a while."

I stretched out on the seat, feeling warm from hearing her voice. My left knee banged the wall but I did not care.

"Hearing you makes this day happy, "

I said, struggling to get clear of the pain-killers. "How is Firenze?"

"Actually, I'm down in Capri now. Semester break from school."

"Me, too," I wisecracked. "But I do miss you, my dear."

"Max, I had to take this job. Just like you had to stay in New York and fight your way back into the Department. How is that going, by the way?"

"The other side is winning."

"Max, the reason that I'm calling is that I think that I've fallen in love."

My body jackknifed in the seat. The trees whipped past my railroad car window. I tried to concentrate on counting them.

"By your tone," I said, "you probably don't mean that you've fallen in love with me."

"Max, can't you give up the smart-alecky talk right now?"

"Now is when I need it."

"I thought that I should notify you of this," she said. "So that we could open a dialogue and make an informed decision about our course of action."

My head shook back and forth.

Wisecracking felt impossible. But I tried.

"You make it sound like my father's appendicitis operation," I said. "I love you, Jody. At the same time, you have to be happy in your Italian life."

"Max, your ideas are just too much for me right now."

My breath jerked inwards.

"I'll call you later," she said.

The cellphone face looked back at me.

A noise came out of my mouth.

It was a small, pained noise.

As usual, I had over-bought on food. My bag bulged.

I gorged on the feta cheese.

"Eating against heartache never works," I muttered. "It just gets me fatter."

My chest drew in and out painfully, slowly.

In the dark window, I could see my throat pulse beating too fast.

"Let the body ease up," I went on. "Avoid Amtrak heart attacks."

Sleep kept slipping away from me.

❧

The train pulled me across Texas.

"Dallas didn't interest me enough to get off," I said to the conductor. "Ditto San Antonio. Waco was raining, so that killed my spirit. I want to go where there is no rain or snow."

"Then you should try El Paso, Albuquerque, Phoenix or Basta, California," he said. "Seems like you're running out of towns. Why didn't you fly?"

"On three days notice? Too expensive. I'm on your special fare, Anywhere, U.S.A. for two-fifty round trip. As long as you keep this car heated, I'm in no hurry."

He looked at me as if I needed special care. It was a look that I knew pretty well.

"Sir, just where do you want to go?"

"No big cities," I said. "What is a 'Basta'? In Italian and other languages, it means 'enough'!"

"Railroad town," he said. "Kind of a sleepy place. Pretty country, if you like dry desert."

"Make sure you wake me before we get to Basta," I said. "That sounds just like what I want."

The pain kept buzzsawing around my left knee.

Stretching out in half-sleep, I dreamed that Jody was curled warmly beside me.

❧

Daylight colored on my window.
The painkillers kept me sleeping.
The window grayed and darkened.
"Basta!"
The window showed daylight.
I shook my face around, crutching down the steps.
It was a train station platform that ran along the tracks. The platform ended and the scrubby pale gold desert started.
The sky shone blue jean colors overhead.
Basta showed blocky adobe buildings with the same desert all around it.
My crutches wheeled me along the platform.

A few cabs clustered near the platform.

Ten minutes of fast New Yorker talk got me riding towards a residence hotel on the outskirts of Basta. The broken and dried wooden sign read "Route 66 Tumbleweed Arms- Residence Rooms by Day, Week or Month."

"Excuse me extremely," I asked the shaved-head, reedy joker behind the desk. A scar cut crossed his face from eyebrow to chin. "But what do you have here?"

"Rented rooms. One, two or three bedrooms. Privy in back that everyone shares. But you might not be able to handle it. The house next door is already full. I rent it to some nuts. But you're all stove-in, crutches, and we get some rough waddies here."

"Sure you do," I said. "Naturally you do. Stands to reason. 'Rough waddies.' Just what is a 'waddie'?"

"Drifter. Just moving on. Something like you are."

Dignity required me to lean on my crutches.

Even to me, I sounded like a wiseguy big city fast-talker.

"Gee, I sure hope that I can give you some money for a single-bed apartment," I said.

"Five-seventy-five a month," he said. "Cash, no checks. I'm Chick, the boss of everything here. Rooms and the houses."

Twenty minutes later, I was staring at a large butter-colored room with three huge windows showing the night desert outside.

The room smelled of spilled beer, cigarettes and fast food grease.

"Our hero finds himself in grim circumstances," I said aloud. "I wonder what Professor Jody would say about this."

As I spoke her name, my head eased down and my shoulders hunched up.

"In order for our hero to stay jolly, he should promenade somewhat."

ℏ

I hauled my beef on crutches in between my building and the one next to it.

Twenty feet of desert ran between them.

A smell like parched grass mixed with dirt flowered the evening. I supposed that it was the scent of the desert.

Last streaks of purpling reddish skies filled the sky.

Through the next building's window, the one Shaven-Head said he rented, an Asian woman frolicked with a thick white dog. She looked beautiful to me. She buried her face in the dog's ruff, caught me looking at both of them and frowned.

Classical music played in her room.

I tried to look harmless. But my whiskers were coming white through my skin and my crazy green glasses bobbed on my nose. I did not look dapper.

I crutched away.

A road sign read "Main Street, Part of the Original Route 66."

Route 66 had its own mythology. It ran from Chicago to Los Angeles. Nat King Cole had sung about it. Other singers followed him. I hummed the lyrics now. Cheering up was needed.

A long stone bridge arced to my left.

A dozen railroad tracks tangled underneath it.

This looked like the oldest part of town.

When the first railroad line came into Basta, the rough-necks probably had slithered off the freight cars to build shanties near the tracks,

A century later, I was copying them.

A stone statue and scrappy yellowed grass formed a kind of square. Locals in cowboy hats and bluejeans hung out there, talking. Guitar music played from somewhere.

As I hobbled onto the square, I breathed in deeply, taking the clean cool air into my Amtrak-ed body.

A bearded ragamuffin with a crown of pure silver hair limped in front of me. He looked about sixty.

"Mister, the sergeant told me to waste some Iraqi civilians," he said. "But I wouldn't do it. He run me up to a court martial."

"You look kind of old for it, sir," I said.

Watching his wide grimy hands, I moved away.

"It was a moral decision," he said.

I stopped.

"Yessir, soldier," I said. "I'm listening to you."

"Now I'm paying for it," he said. "Stockade, Dishonorable Discharge, six years hard labor-"

"Okay. You win."

My fingers slipped my wallet from my bluejeans back pocket.

He came in closer and bumped onto me.

"Hey!" I said.

His boot hit my shin and then the crutch.

I went sprawling down onto the square. Both crutches hit my ribs. My head slammed against the statue's base.

His foot smashed my face.

He yanked the wallet from my hand.

"Give me a hand here!" I shouted, not thinking.

None of the locals moved.

They watched.

"People!" I said from the ground. It sounded like pleading.

The ragamuffin with my wallet looked like someone's grandpappy. He was not dangerous.

But nobody moved to stop him or help me up.

The ragamuffin and my wallet went down a lane.

"Basta is afraid of harmless grandpappy muggers?" I said out loud. "This town got trouble."

CHAPTER 2

My Big Idea

Guitar music filigreed over from the next house.

> I remember Grandma tellin' me
> That I was born
> As the sun was comin' up,
> Early in the morn'.

Coffee and bacon smells wafted over to my bloody nose. It drove me rampant with hunger.

Alone in this boxy room, healing would take forever. I needed distractions. My neighbors seemed lively enough to distract anyone.

"I wonder who that woman is," I said aloud. "At my age, I am acting like a teenager, knocking on a door to find a new love."

Clawing in my backpack, I looked at my Mediterranean food kit.

The tempting cooking smells got stronger.

We tenants shared a bathroom and a tin shower. Blue-bottle bruises marked my face. My left eye looked like a To-mato Surprise. Shaving for the first time in more than a week, my face looked younger and cleaner.

My wardrobe did the best possible to my eyes.

The crutches might grow some sympathy in this hustle.

The house next door was adobe, gnarled and cracked by age. Its window frames of were stained oxblood, like the ones in my room. A stucco sign said "Private Residence." It looked solid and cozy. The tenants would not have to share a shower like I did. Three jalopies from the nineteen-fifties lay between the apartments and Main Street. You could not tell if they were trash or decoration.

Following the guitar music, I knuckled my neighbor's door.

"Who?" a man's voice sounded from inside.

My feet twitched to run away. But I remembered the woman from last night, mumbling that faint heart never won fair maiden.

I sucked in a deep breath and bellowed back.

"I'm Max Royster, your new neighbor from across the way," I said. My tenor voice climbed and broke. "Got some exquisite breakfast foodstuffs that I cannot use."

I was expecting a man to open the door.

But a woman with cornflower blue eyes under a shock of white hair eased out the cracked wooden door out. She scrutinized me.

"Would you like to see my teeth?" I asked.

She smiled and changed her face. The switch dazzled me. She was no longer a flinty watchman but a carefree teenager with shining lips and eyes.

Behind her, a collection of slim youngsters in their twenties were brunching away on bagels and omelets.

I needed to give her some material.

"I been carrying this food across America," I said. "Jars of imported olive oil and the healthiest hummus you could imagine. Canned dolmas grape leaves."

Her mouth quirked. She was interested.

"You have to help me eat this stuff before it goes bad," I rattled on.

"We can do that," a gangly athletic fellow behind her said. "Damn betcha. Some of us are always hungry."

Behind them, the Asian woman from last night brought the thick white dog out from her room. She did not look at me.

"And I just moved in," I said.

"Some stuff spoils unless we pitch in and consume it," I said.

"How did you carry all this on crutches?" the woman asked.

"I am very balanced," I said.

I wanted her to see me as a goofy dreamer but harmless.

She made a decision and opened the door wider.

"I am Zygolt," she said. "The ramrod in this outfit. Come and join us."

"My name's Marcus," the athlete said.

He sported curly black hair cut short over a hungry face with large staring eyes. Something about him drew my attention.

"Some people call me an actor."

"Let me know where you're acting," I said. "I clap real loud."

It was time to keep playing it dumb. They should accept me as their crutchy new neighbor.

"You're college roommates?" I asked.

"No," Zygolt said. "My stars and garters. I look that young? Trying to start some cultural awareness in Basta. I'm a modern dancer."

"Banding together for morale and protection," Marcus said. "And cash loans. We have actors and dancers and even a dog trainer."

"I can figure out who is the dog trainer," I said, giving it my best and most boyish smile at the Asian woman.

She lifted her face towards me but did not react beyond that. As she turned her eyes towards me, I shifted my weight on the crutches towards her. My foodstuffs swung in my shoulder bag.

"That's Koy," Marcus said. "With Snowball-the-Wonder-Dog."

"Here, sit down before you fall down, Max," Zygolt said. "And eat with us artists-"

"The demimonde," I said. "The half-world of defrocked priests, mad poets, politicians-in-hiding, street hustlers and more."

"Whoever we are. I sometimes wonder. Tell us about your injuries."

"You are," I said, searching for the right word, "'Showbizzers.' Artists with something to sell."

"But nobody's buying," a wiry spider of a woman, red-haired, with a pointed chin, said. "I'm Clytemnestra since nobody around here has the manners to introduce me."

We ate together.

"What did you call us again?" Marcus asked.

"Showbizzers."

"Tell us about your leg, Max. Get real. Are you on the lam after cracking cribs in Hell's Kitchen?"

I looked at him.

"I played Detective Callaghan in *Detective Story*," Marcus said. "Two seasons in Las Vegas summer stock. I make a pretty good cop."

I plunged into my operation and last night's goat rodeo mess with the mugger. Koy, the Asian woman, never showed much reaction. Maybe she was sedated on heavy-duty Quaaludes. Otherwise, my charm would melt her.

"That's outrageous, Max," Zygolt said. "Wait until you try reporting it to those jackass San Risa County deputies."

"He got all my ID," I said. "Deputy's report should get me temporary papers."

"You don't know those damn fools," Zygolt said. "They'll tell you to call the Basta city cops. That it happened there. So they don't have to pick up a pen."

"The old reliable, huh?"

"They are just guests on the county rolls," she said. "Took me thirty-two mother-kissing years of dance, diet and practice to get where I am now. We dancers risk injuries that could cripple us. Just like other athletes."

"Or we ignore our doctors," Clytemnestra, the red-haired woman said.

"All of us learn our craft that way. If those deputies struggled like us, they would know the value of work. They would serve us citizens."

Munching Egyptian baked flatbread with hummus and olives, I thought that over.

Then the idea struck me.

I swallowed and leaned forward.

"I've got it!" I said. "What a wiggy wild idea."

The Showbizzers stared at me.

"You just said it yourself, Zygolt," I said. "Use Showbizzers and their skills to fight crime."

Nobody moved.

They just stared.

"I know it will work," I said. "It's the best idea I ever had."

Chapter 3

My Big Idea Dead and Buried

"Why would we want to play cops-and-robbers?" Zygolt asked. "Our lives as artists are already nuts. Pure crazy. Why should we take on more risks by playing kid detective games?"

"It's vigilante thinking," Marcus said.

"And against the damn law."

"Do you think that you'll turn vigilante?" I asked.

"Does anyone, beforehand?" he asked. "I'm Jewish. My grandparents suffered Fascism. It began with vigilantes in Italy."

Nobody's faces looked happy or open with my idea. They just looked at me as they ate. Snowball maintained a neutral expression.

"Bite me," Marcus said. "What a dumb idea."

"Zygolt," Koy said. "I'll pick up the groceries later at the Desert Market."

"Cool," Zygolt said. "Max, drop your idea."

"In the damn privy," Marcus said. "Deep."

"Police gotta go to academies," Clytemnestra said. "Learn shooting, the law and how to milk the system. Without that training, you just have a mob. Your idea would just unleash that same mob on the people."

"Except that you would not carry guns," I said. "So, there's no need to learn shooting. You'll use your minds, your creative thinking, the way you do now as Showbizzers to handle problems. You don't arrest people or execute search warrants, so legal training is brief. You would just have to learn about privacy and what you cannot do. Showbizzers, let's crush crime."

"We cannot do this," Zygolt said. "That's clear to me. And I'm the boss witch here."

"Just think about it," I said.

Part of me was excited by this idea. My chest tightened and my left arm tingled. Those were the usual signs.

"This is a new county," Clytemnestra said. "Used to be San Bernardino County. But that was just too big. So they created this new county, San Risa County, to make things more efficient. What a joke. But it's not working. We're on our own, kids."

Koy and her big white dog Snowball went into their room.

"Now that I've dazzled you with good food and new ideas," I said. "I'm going to slide on out."

"Max, your ideas are crazy," Marcus said. "Amusing but crazy."

"Didn't you enjoy playing a cop on stage?" I asked. "How would you feel cracking real cases and helping real victims?"

With a big glad-hand wave, I left.

They might dismiss my proposal. But my idea drew me more and more.

☙

Another thought struck me back in my room. An image of Koy and the dog danced before me.

"Must be puppy-love," I sang, off-key.

To put my plan into action, I locked my door and crutched out towards Main Street.

An aging cowboy type in broken-grained denim shirt, jacket and jeans was ankling along Main Street.

"Excuse me, sir," I asked. "Where is the Desert Market, please?"

He gawked at me and kept walking.

"I mean it," I said.

He did not stop.

"Basta loves me," I said.

Two more worthies ignored me.

A third one stopped and pointed. He had a left eye purpling under someone's fist and a tattoo of a dragon along his neck. Scabs bloomed on his own left-hand knuckles, from jabbing another fool, probably over nothing.

"The Desert Market is right down here," he said. "About two miles. I guess you're new here."

Being a Californian, he figured that I was spinning through life in some snappy sports car. He never thought that I might walk.

A New Yorker would say "Buddy, it's 'aboutafortyfi' minud walk there from heah."

So I was hatching a plan and it involved walking a bit. The crutches poked against my armpits.

After ten days, they still pained me.

Basta's tangle of streets lay before me. To my left, the bridge spanned high above the railroad tracks.

This was Basta's Old Town. The square where the wino robbed me looked virginal in the daylight.

Beyond that, sun-shadowed mountains rose up against the sandy desert ground.

The sight broke a smile against my lips, thinking of icy drizzle coming down on the IRT subway tracks in Manhattan's January.

This was better.

My feet swung under the crutches.

Up ahead, a bearded dude in a work shirt stamped "Hospitality Pays" kicked another man in the groin. The second man squealed but kept throwing clumsy jabs. He wore a torn mustard-colored T-shirt, bluejeans and what looked like snakeskin cowboy boots.

Lots of brawlers kept fighting after a groin kick. It only turned them madder. Mister Cowboy Boots seemed like one of those.

He circled Hospitality, ducked some slow punches, took one on his shoulder and threw a left hook.

The hook hit Hospitality and rocked him. Boots jabbed him but missed.

They were fighting about thirty feet ahead of me, in the parking lot of a car upholstery place. A growing crowd of working-types moved back gave them room on the asphalt.

"It's all about the friendship!" Boots shouted. "That's all, bro!"

Hospitality was too busy throwing strikes to answer. None of them hit.

"Beat each other silly," I muttered. "This cowboy's a-courting Lady Koy."

My wooden crutches spiraled me closer to the fighting fools.

Hospitality slopped against a parked Ford and spilled down onto the concrete. Boots kicked out and then down. His heel caught Hospitality's chin.

The head went limp and then flopped back against the ground. Boots stomped again. Something pink and pulpy smeared his glossy boot.

The ex-cop in me shouted a warning. Boots could kill Hospitality that way.

"Hey, hey!" I shouted. "Nice fighting there, my man. You won it!"

Boots kept stomping.

"That talk works back home," I said. "What's with these cowboys here?"

To break his thoughts, I swiveled my crutches so that I was coming closer.

"Hey, you're gonna hold up traffic!" I said. "And my girl's picking me up. You trying to gack up my social life or something?"

"Shut up, you cuckoo!" one of the crowd said. "Let them fight!"

"That's all they know," another put in.

It was time to keep winging and slinging it.

"What about my private life?" I said, clowning for the crowd. Sometimes you had to entertain them more than anything else. It worked that way in Patrol.

This audience was sitting on their hands.

Boots kept kicking. Hospitality tried to roll away. Another car tire stopped him.

"Forget that old thing!" A woman shouted.

At last, somebody was talking back to me.

"I'd like to!" I hammed back. "It's depressing. But it's the only one that I got. All I got left is a few jokes."

I was setting myself up for the audience. But they did not take the bait.

"A few jokes!" I repeated.

"Yeah and you're one of them!" another woman shouted.

"Hey, hey!" I said. "Who said that? That's the crime of Elder Abuse right there. That's against the law, you!"

The idea was to break up their concentration.

"You characters cool all this noise!" I told Boots and Hospitality. "You're messing up my Saturday!"

Somebody had to jump in and correct me. They always did.

"Today's Wednesday!" a man crowed.

"Yeah, but the plan for Saturday starts today!" I said.

"That don't make no sense!"

"No!" I clowned back. "It's that Sunday morning that don't make no sense."

Boots bobbed near me and threw a punch. He looked like he was forgetting Hospitality.

My heart hammered. This stuff always scared me.

Like every street cop, I wondered if this would be The One-That-Stops-Me-Forever.

But I was in it now. I could not run. But I wanted to.

"Yo, homes!" someone hollered from the crowd. "Stay in the game, there."

Everyone needed an out.

I wanted to give him one.

"He can't stay in that game!" I shouted. "He got me to deal with."

"What are you, anyway?" Boots said. "Look like a pile of sad turd."

I half-turned to my audience.

"Rather blunt fellow, that," I said.

Nobody reacted.

"This is a tough audience," I said.

"You can't break this up!" a slat-thin studious type hollered at me. He swung a work-scarred hand in my direction.

Like an amateur, he let the hand hang there.

I stepped closer, put my left crutch end on his toe and pressed down with all my weight. With my right, I grabbed his hand.

He tried pulling back. He could not move his trapped foot. He tried punching but I twisted his wrist outward and locked it.

I lifted the left crutch and stabbed down on his foot with the right one. He yelped and dropped to the ground.

"Crutch-fighting," I panted. "I just invented it."

The fight lay dead. I had done my job.

"How come you so hateful with cowboys?" a small white-haired gnome of a woman asked.

I looked down at the joker I had put down.

"That's a cowboy?" I asked.

"What else?"

"Doesn't look like any cowboy I ever saw," I said.

"And where did you ever see a goddamned cowboy? On TV? Riding through the screen?"

"You're right," I said.

"Then why you down on us?" another man puffing on a cigar under his handlebar moustache asked.

"I'm not," I said. "Listen up."

I sucked in a breath and sang:

"From this valley, they say you are going,
I will miss your sweet face and your smile,
Just because you are weary and tired,
You are changing your range for a while."

"That's a cowboy song," I said. "'Red River Valley'."

"We'll catch you someplace else!" a woman shouted in a beery smoker's voice. "Settle your hash."

"Where I come from in New York," I said, "prejudice against cowboys is not a hot topic. We have other prejudices to fret about."

"New York!" another woman bellowed. "Get a rope!"

"East meets West," I told myself, spinning away.

Knowing better than to look back at the crowd, I kept up a brisk pace with my crutches and gained the next rise in the road.

The same smell of grass drying and hot sand wafted around me. It was the desert smell that I was getting used to.

I kept hobbling.

Jeeps and pickups bounced past me.

Then the same Jeep from next door rolled up. The driver's glossy black hair marked her as Koy. Snowball-the-Wonder-Dog leaned his white curly head out of the window.

Koy's eyes connected with mine. She looked at me. She kept driving.

Chapter 4

Paid Professionals

Koy passed in her Jeep; I pitched forward and fell on top of my crutches.

My bruises keened. Vessels of new pain split open under my eyes.

"'Froggy Woggy goes a-wooing'," I muttered. "This is loving up the hard way."

Cars wharrumphed past me. A motorcycle burped in my ear.

Some fast-driving fool might hit me.

My cop sense told me to get moving somewhere.

Another engine with a coughy muffler wheezed closer.

I rolled over. It would fool nobody.

Koy looked at me from the Jeep's steering wheel.

Her brown eyes drilled at me under her tangled crown of raven hair.

She was looking right through me.

So was fluffy white Snowball-the -Wonder-Dog.

"Get in," was all that she said.

"Our first conversation together," I said under my breath. "What memorable opening words you utter."

She ground the gears.

It sounded like a hurry-up call.

My crutches and I clambered into the back seat. Snowball did not look as though he was planning to step aside graciously.

"Shih-Shih," I said in my broken Mandarin.

"What do you want?" she said. "I worked this out in grad school. Whenever a man says something sweet to a woman, he must want something."

"I said 'shih-shih'. That phrase is not sweet."

"I don't speak Mandarin," Koy said. "But I know that 'shih-shih' means 'thank you' in Mandarin. I'm from Guang Zhou. We prefer Cantonese. We fight against speaking Mandarin."

"Sorry."

"You look it," she said, her Chinese accent slurring her words. When Koy got riled, like now, I could tell that English was not her first language. Her words dipped and rolled. Somehow, it charmed me into smiling. "Where can I drop you off?"

"But I just went down!"

"Ha!"

"I'm a beaten man," I said. "I've got to report my robbery to the local cops."

"Why not use the phone?"

"They need my fingers signing the report, they said. And they're too busy for sending a patrol car to take it."

She tossed her glossy black hair over a slim shoulder. Snowball slopped his pink tongue across the head cushion. I would not be using that cushion for a while.

"There's a sheriff's substation in the mall," she said. "I'll drop you there."

"There's always the return trip."

She did not answer.

"Are you looking for clever ways to spend time with me?" I asked.

'Another man myth," she said. "Craparoo."

"You're looking at me," I said. "Are you admiring.... the body?"

She kept her eyes on the highway.

"You want to get someone from Guangzhou angry," she said, "speak Mandarin to them."

"Why is that?" I asked.

She just stroked Snowball with a thin hand.

We moved along Basta's motel strip. One boasted a 1950s neon sign reading "The Original Route 66 Hangout." Vintage cars cluttered the sandy grass in front of the motel.

"Are we near Route 66?" I asked.

She shot me a look as if I were unworthy of speech.

"We're on the goddamn Main Street," she said. "Main Street IS Route 66."

"Can you help me get inside the police station?" I asked. "These crutches form impossibility."

"It's a sheriff's substation and, no, I can't," she said. "And won't. Don't trust police or sheriffs or anything like that. Too much government control."

"But I'm a victim."

"You certainly act like one. My goodness gracious."

"You said that you don't like the government, the police," I said. "I'm not wild about most of them, either. Why give them the satisfaction of seeing me fall into their station? It's better if they see that you and I stand united against them."

"Boy, I never heard such craparoo."

"Is this a Cantonese expression?" I asked.

"I left Guangzhou when I was 12. Okay. I can't stand to hear a man whine."

"You're looking at me," I said. "Are you admiring –"

"No."

She pulled the Jeep into a strip mall with half the stores papered up and going out of business. Lease signs scarred the doorways. The trashcans overflowed.

At the strip's end stood a smallish adobe building with the words "San Risa County Sheriff / Basta Substation" on the wall.

Wheeling my crutches under my arms, I went in as Koy held the door. Snowball watched us from the front passenger seat. He seemed to disapprove.

∾

A front desk stood before us.

Young crew cut deputies in tan uniforms and shellacked black leather gunbelts busied themselves with phones and forms.

They eyed Koy and me.

"Good morning," I said, trying on a winning smile. "I was robbed last night."

A deputy standing about six feet-five with a broken nose and premature gray hair walked past me.

I repeated the same words.

He kept walking and vanished around a corner.

"Basta is afraid of harmless grandpappy muggers? This town got trouble."

I sighed and squeezed my eyes shut.

"It's going to be a difficult campaign," I said. "They're going to make it one."

"Well?" Koy demanded. "Are you going to report this or not?"

Indulging myself, I looked her over for a second and then heaved a great sigh.

A freckle-faced deputy with an elongated head looked up from his desk.

"Someone beat and robbed me last night," I said again.

"Why didn't you report it last night?" he asked.

"I was hurt."

"Call an ambulance?"

"Too discouraged to."

"So you're coming in to report this now?"

I took in his essence with my eyes. He probably did great on pull-ups, the two-mile shuttle run and handgun qualification. He would score high on everything that I did poorly. Trainers would smile when they saw his scores. But he had lost his way somewhere, forgetting that a cop served the public.

Koy was taking this all in and shaking her shapely head.

"Don't be eyeballing me," he said. "Let me see some ID."

"The rascals took it last night. I'll give you my name and d/o/b and you can run me through New York Motor Vehicles."

Bit by painful bit, he dragged me through the report form.

In New York, I had suffered through partners like this. They made for long days.

The deputies ogled Koy, stuck their thumbs in their gunbelts and strutted a bit before her. High school boys will be boys.

My deputy shuffled paper, checked his computer and kept struggling through the form.

One deputy, a squat Latino with his hair parted in the middle and forearms like knotted tree branches, left the substation and came back.

"That your Jeep outside?" he asked me.

His tone put me to answering slowly.

"Nossir," I said.

"Then how did you get here, all crippled up like you are?"

"It's a gift," I said.

"Because that dog inside doesn't have a license on him. And that's a town ordinance violation right there. Missy, is that your car?"

He was pointing at Koy and asking her.

It seemed like deputy needed to show his sergeant some summons activity on undocumented hounds like Snowball. Prowling the parking lot where victims had to park was safer than patrolling Basta's back alleys.

Koy ignored him.

He repeated the question.

"Do you have a restroom here?" she asked.

"By the filing cabinet, there."

Koy arose, walked over near the front door and left through the door without saying a word.

"Where's she going?" my deputy asked.

"Wherever she wants," I said. "You know today's women."

"What's your craft back there in New York? Your job?"

"Unemployed."

"Yeah. That goddamn well figures. Sorry as you look."

"How sweet a pleasantry," I said.

"Whatever. Use this slip of paper as your temporary ID. Have a nice day."

Gaining back the outdoors with the thick mountains in the distance, I started hobbling back home.

ᴇᴏ

After some scattered minutes of pain, Koy and Snowball pulled up in the Jeep. I fell back into my spot in the back seat.

"Do you see what I mean?" I asked. "Don't you think that you and your showbizzer friends could take that report better?"

"Snowball could."

She pulled out onto the street.

"What's that word you just used?" she asked. "Showbizzers?"

"That's you. And your group. Dog trainers like you, dancers, actors, poets and musicians. You are all in show business, whether you admit it or not."

"Tell that to Snowball. Why do you care so much about your new idea? That you would want some of us to risk our lives to prove you right. Is your ego that big?"

"I'm afraid so."

Chapter 5

My Big Idea Dug Up and Smothered Again

"What you're doing doesn't make sense," Zygolt said the next morning during breakfast.

"It does to me," I said. "So I'm crafting something out of nothing. It is a something that speaks to me. You're an artist. Isn't that the definition of art?"

"Nobody knows what art is."

"I do," I said. "Art is what everyone in high school was doing. And promising to do forever. But we got distracted."

"We didn't!" Clytemnestra beamed, doing a Yoga warm-up.

"And you're not more than eight years out of high school," I said.

"Damn, man. You're holding my age against me?"

"To be an actress at twenty-two means being twenty-two," I said. "To be an actress at fifty-two means being an actress."

"Just the point." Zygolt fixed me with her cobalt-blue eyes. "We theater fools got no damn security. Marcus could acquire Chronic Fatigue Syndrome. Koy an allergy to dog hair. Why should we take on more risks by playing cops and robbers?"

The others, stretching after eating their breakfast, nodded. Their limbs writhed under their clothes.

Koy bounced out of her room. She held the lunging Snowball by the neck. Snowball opened his jaws and drooled joyously.

"Koy, you look wonderful," I said.

She dropped her own smile.

"What do you want?" she asked.

"Me?" I sputtered. "Whatever do you mean?"

"Remember? Whenever a man compliments you, he wants something. So, when you say that to me, I need to know what you want."

Anger slurred her words again.

"But, Max, you digress," Zygolt said.

"I do," I said. "Sorry."

"Despite your boy-meets-goddamn-girl digression, I still wanna know," Zygolt said. "Why should we artists take on play-acting as cops when making a living as an artist is flipping near impossible?"

"Maybe because crime is America's biggest domestic problem," I said. "And we should do something about that."

"I will," Clytemnestra said. "I plan to leave it."

"Will that help things?"

"It'll help me. Going to Thailand and leave all this mess behind."

"How many of us can do that?" I asked. "The other Basta folks, call them 'Bastas', must do laundry at night, walk from the Desert Market to their car and listen for someone's heel scraping behind them. Nobody needs to live in that kind of fear."

"Most do," she said.

"Not now. Nationwide, that is changing. Because smarter, more committed types are getting more involved with policing."

"Don't think that they are smarter or more anything," she said. "I see them as bored, toxic, fat persons who want to play vigilante."

She looked at my stomach.

"It's too late for me to try sucking that in," I said. "The ship has sailed."

"You could lose some weight," she said. "What do you plan to do about that?"

"Nothing."

"Nothing?"

"Perhaps less."

"Aw, bite me, Max," Marcus the actor said. "Your idea blows."

"Says which?" I asked.

"Why does this matter so much to you?" Marcus asked. He was palming the floor. "Is there some dark reason that you want to create young vigilantes out of us?"

"No dark or mysterious reason," I said. "It just seems worthwhile to me."

"We actors always say 'break a leg'," Marcus said. "Means give a striking, no-holds-barred performance. But your idea can get my whole damn body broke up. No thanks."

"Sounds fishy," Clytemnestra said. She was doing a split on the floor and her hair played out against black leotards.

"And I don't agree that crime is America's worst problem," Marcus said. "Never been robbed or burglarized, but the economy is still kicking my butt."

"All our butts," Koy said. "We do a luxury service when everyone thinks about necessities."

"The economy's the problem!" Zygolt said. "Mother-kissing politicians."

"Come on, Showbizzers," I said.

"And you're an amateur about crime," Zygolt said. "A dilettante, almost. Don't got any training or skills in policing, right?"

"Just logic," I said. "I know that my idea will work."

The room grew quiet.

"Come on, Showbizzers," I said. "Break a leg. And crush crime."

She did not smile now.

"Just for the sake of argument," she said, "how do we know that you are not just a dreamer who will get some of us killed?"

I could not answer that.

Once again, it was "we" scrutinizing me and seeing me as flawed. It had been like that on the cops, too.

"Well, that's our show for today," I said. "Street theater taught me a good exit line when I hear one."

My crutches twirled under my arms.

Nobody asked me to stay.

To walk off my mad, I kept going down Main Street. Pickups burped past. I tried not to think.

"Break a leg," I said. "And crush crime."

My talk had only alienated the Showbizzers. They would peg me as some kind of nut.

Maybe they were right.

A loose nest of tramps and losers clumped around the Desert Market parking lot. Their skins held the red burnished tang of heavy sun exposure. Some of their eyes burned very blue above their beards.

Their crusted denim or cracked leather jackets lay alongside them. They needed them for the frosty desert nights.

These characters would hitchhike long stretches between Basta and Los Vegas. When they were flush, they might rent rooms near mine in Basta. My neighborhood would draw them.

The trek down here had tuckered me out. The strong sun tightened. Pulling my crutches behind me, I rested under a big shade tree.

My lids closed.

I dropped off to sleep.

❧

When I woke up, the drifters were cackling over a six-pack of Budweiser in their midst. One played the harmonica. The tune sounded like "Dixie." They might be Good Old Boys from the Heartland of America.

Mouth dry and dusty, I tried getting up on my crutches. But my left leg had gone to sleep with me and numbed up. When I put weight on it, I stumbled, lost my grip on the crutch and sagged downwards.

A Latino family pushed their shopping cart near me. The kids gawked at me falling, giggling and shouting in Spanish.

The father, fattish and graying, opened up his station wagon tailgate and stowed groceries inside.

"Can't you funky smelly bums drink somewhere else?" he said, hauling more bags. "Trailer trash."

Like a fool, I looked around. Then I realized that he was talking to me.

"What do you mean?" I asked.

"Drink and carry on somewhere else," he said.

The drifters ignored him.

"Me?" I asked.

My hands fought to get on the crutches again. They shook from anger.

"All of you bums," he said.

The drifters were just about twenty feet from me. He saw us as one big group.

"I'm not with them!" I blurted out.

He made a face and turned back to his family.

The drifters were cutting up another six-pack, can by can.

The "Whoosh!" of pressurized cans filled the air.

The family father had been right. They did look like me. We could be part of the same shambling, colorful group.

CHAPTER 6

Government Believes Mostly in Lunch

The weather stayed warmish through the next week.

I got into the habit of crutching down to the Desert Market parking lot every morning. It gave me a kind of fitness routine. My arms thickened and grew stronger from the crutches.

The drifters tried bumming cigarettes or change. When that did not work, they left me alone.

The Showbizzers greeted me in passing. But they did not invite me over for breakfast. Koy seemed distant when she walked Snowball around the houses.

When the January weather let me, I lolled under the trees, remembering patrol in Brooklyn.

As the sun was setting, I would make my way back home. Daylight kept me safer from the car traffic along Main Street.

On Friday afternoon, I was stretched out under my favorite tree near the parking lot.

A Toyota lurched through the parking lot, turned the corner and kept going.

Ten minutes later, the same car came back and parked.

Then they left.

They came back a third time. One man left the Toyota, entered the market and came out a few minutes later.

The car left.

Now I was paying attention.

If I ran a team of hoods planning to rob the Desert Market, I would surely check out the parking lot and area beforehand.

Hobbling away from my pals so as not to inhibit them, I leaned on the right crutch and fished out my cellphone and thumbed 911.

"San Risa County 911," a woman's twangy voice said. "Where is the emergency?"

"In Basta. At the Desert Market. Toyota Celica, green. Four-door, wire rim wheels. Dent on rear driver's side bumper," I said. "Paper temporary plate in the back. Four men inside, twenties to thirties. Gringo white-type guy driving. Silver wristwatch left wrist. Latino man passenger in the front seat. Moustache, balding, about thirty-five. He went inside the Desert Market, bought nothing and left with his pals. Is this all on tape?"

"All our calls are taped," she said, leaving out the word "sir."

"Good. My name is Max Royster, living at 42317 Main Street, here in Basta. I'm an ex-cop."

"What are these men doing? There is no emergency."

"Today is Friday," I said. "Payday for most. Prime robbery time is Friday afternoon. They've cruised this parking lot without stopping three times already. Toyotas get stolen more than any other car. Does California DMV keep track of paper temporary plates?"

"I can't really say," she said.

"Because New York does not track temporary licenses. New York DMV just passes them out. That makes this Toyota the perfect robbery car. And two of the suspects in the car are Latino."

"How does that matter?" she asked. Her voice slurred and sharpened. She sounded as if she was offended because she was Latina herself.

"Because I'm new here in California," I said. "And, from what I see, Latinos and gringos do not mix socially that much. They blend more in New York."

"You remember that this line is tape-recorded?" she asked.

"Then excuse this sociology. But Latinos and gringos here mostly mix for work here. Or crime. They may be planning to rob this the Desert Market. I'm standing by with pictures of the car and suspects from my phone."

"I can't send a unit out for this," she said.

"Maybe not. But you should."

She let that hang in the air.

"At least, put on a notice on the radio about the Toyota," I said. "So your deputies can do an investigative stop."

"We would have no legal right to stop it, sir."

I blew out a breath and sagged against the wall.

The winter afternoon was cooling off now. Winds strengthened. Tonight would chill us all.

"This Being-A-Good-Citizen routine wearies me greatly," I said. "From what I see from my crutches, every driver in Southern California breaks at least one traffic law every twenty seconds that he drives. A deputy who sees that violation can stop the car."

"Are you telling us how to do our job?" she asked.

"Somebody should."

"Sir, you can be arrested for misuse of the 911 system," she said. "I'm terminating the call now."

I gave my name, address again.

But she had already hung up.

Chapter 7

Gunning Up

After that chat with the halls of power, I had to do something.

So I crutched to the two pawnshops in Basta and shopped.

"Yep," the dealer said. "Your rent receipt makes you a California resident. Check it out. What kind of gun are you looking to buy?"

"You got everything in God's kingdom here," I said, trying to grease up the pawnbroker for a low price. I will never learn. "Is that a cowboy gun?"

"Colt Peacemaker 1881 model.45 Long Colt by Vaquero," he said. "Check it out. The Gun-that-Won-the-West. The balance and frame are so good that you can hit a man at sixty feet."

"And derringers, too?" I said, crafting a New York accent onto my words.

I wanted him to see me as a rank outsider, fresh off the Greyhound. Which I was.

"I never saw a derringer before," I said. "Outside of the movies, that is."

"Gamblers liked to have one like this —"

He indicated a small pistol, three inches long, double-barreled, with wood grips.

"– tucked up a sleeve," he said. "Or inside a boot-top. If things got hairy, the gambler could put a.41 slug right into the problem. They are small but derringers work well."

"Other than that, Mrs. Lincoln," I said, "how did you enjoy the play?"

"We got the best selection of vintage handguns in San Risa County," he said. Rose-pink glasses slid down his narrow nose. He looked like an actor in a soap opera, with stagy white hair and brows, icy blue eyes and a sculpted chin. Maybe he had been a Showbizzer himself before.

"Have I seen you in films?" I asked. "You look very familiar."

"I messed around with B movies for a while," he said.

"Until you decided that it was time to grow up and sell out?"

"Cowboy bit parts did not pay the bills. Property like this does."

"You're a smart actor," I said. "Look at all these guns! I was thinking about something to protect myself. Like a double-barrel shotgun."

The trick was to get him wanting to sell me what I wanted. Let him think that he had snookered me.

"Double-barrels are outmoded," he said. "And they are rarer than pump-actions. For real protection, you need a bargain-priced little 12-gauge pumper. Like this. From the locker here."

He hefted a worn chunk of burnished nickel and dark stained wood.

"That looks like tooth marks on that stock there," I said.

"Probably are!" he horse-laughed. "Lot of history on this old piece, I bet. Ranny who needed killing."

"I keep forgetting," I said. "Just what is a 'ranny', pray tell?"

"A 'ranny' is a worthless bum trying to be a cowboy but can't cut the mustard. It's a term that the old folks use."

"More cowboy slang, huh?" I said.

"Every fricking loudmouth talks about 'assault rifles'," he said. He leered, twisting that actor's face. "But an assault weapon shoots one bullet at a time. Any time that you trigger a shotgun, nine fricking pellets of.33 caliber fly downrange. Check it out. Pull it five times fast and that shoots out forty-five pellets of double-ought buck. That can turn over a car."

"Gee whiz," I said, choosing a clean-cut All-American Boy turn of phrase, "that sounds expensive. But I'm worried about my neighbors breaking into my place."

"Ninety bucks buys it for you," he said. "I'm losing cash on the deal, but a man needs to protect himself."

This man did.

The movie star pawnbroker also sold me a kicked-around camera. Slinging both the camera and the shotgun into a duffle bag on my shoulder, I could still hobble around on my crutches.

☙

So that's how Sunday morning found me.

My tramp buddies were not there. Perhaps they were kneeling and chanting at Divine Services, contemplating the imponderables.

Using the Sunday edition of a newspaper called *The Desert Dispatch*, I made myself as comfortable as possible lying down on the paper. It protected me from the scrubby desert grass and prickers.

I chose my spot near two metal dumpsters bulging fatly with desert trash. If the robbers hit the Desert Market, I might have to annoy them with the shotgun. Once annoyed, they might get rude with me. They might shoot back. If that should occur, I wanted the dumpsters as bullet protection. Nothing would get through their metal.

To pass time, I thought up reasons for the Showbizzers to see my vision and dabble in policing. Then I remembered the arguments that they had against my idea. They had logic on their side.

I did not.

I seldom did.

Maybe I could outthink them into agreeing with me.

☙

After four hours of dullness, I broke the stakeout creed and hobbled off to wolf down some beef tacos with green chili sauce and cilantro.

They tasted great.

Maybe I should stake out restaurants instead of supermarkets. I could protect the kitchen.

The Desert Market stayed open until eight p.m. on Sunday. That made ten hours on this half-baked stakeout.

The next three days followed like that.

This was starting to feel like a job.

By the market, the drifters kept up their country talk.

"That boy Apgar hit that softball a lick that wouldn't kill a gnat," one of the drifters twanged.

"That Apgar boy is worthless," another agreed. "Word is, he's all hat and no cattle."

"Whatever that means," I muttered. "These good old boys are trying to sound more country than the last speaker."

"I hear that Apgar used to be a deputy and threw his weight around," a new speaker with a red bandana around his bald head said. "Until that old boy Crosswaite shamed him and he quit. Now Apgar's digging roads for the County."

"Crosswaite punked Apgar, and now Apgar don't talk much. Quiet, more humble. And not stealing like so many of our boys around here do."

"Can you see fit to blame them?" another said with a lisp. "Look at our economy."

"You don't have to steal."

"Listen to you! I suppose you grew that leather jacket from a calf."

"I was cold."

"Shoot, I've been truly cold. But never enough to steal."

"Sometimes you got to."

"Street people talk the same everywhere," I said to myself. "It sounds like the talk at Brooklyn Central Booking, in the mugger cage. The only difference is the Western twang with some of them."

As the Desert Market closed, I kept watching. Some takeoff artists liked to hit a market at closing time.

Closing time took forever to arrive.

Koy's Jeep bounced past the Desert Market a couple of times. Snowball's white crown of curls jutted from the window.

Another car, a bluish-green Pinto would stop across Main Street. Marcus the actor had tooled around in that same car. Maybe he had recognized me and wondered why I was lolling around near those drifters.

I could imagine him telling the Showbizzers. It would sound something like "Hey, guys, I saw that fat old windbag

Max pounding down beers with the beer-drinkers at the Desert Market. Are we dealing with an alcohol abuser who conceals his drinking behind grandiose schemes and narcissistic talk?"

Cheery talk like that might follow.

No restaurants stayed open late between the Desert Market and home. So I would pull myself home hungry.

❧

At home, I slumped down on my rented bed.

"Why are you doing this stakeout nonsense, Maxy?" I would ask myself under the scratchy wool blanket. "Transients like you often wind up talking to themselves out loud. And then they fashion themselves into colorful Western characters in desert towns like Basta."

My neighbors the Showbizzers stayed up late. Fried food smells mixed with marijuana as they talked late into the night.

"Tomorrow, I quit this tomfoolery," I said. "If these whiz-bang deputies and Showbizzers don't care about robbery and mayhem, why should I?"

❧

The next morning bloomed windy and grayish outside the Desert Market. I did not know why I was there.

"I'm going, going, gone," I kept telling myself. "Out of here."

The drifters were settling around the shaded side of the Desert Market.

The Toyota rolled inside the parking lot. Men shapes filled the windows.

Nerves made me fumble. I banged the duffle bag against my left crutch, almost knocking myself down.

They drove to the red zone in front of the Desert Market. All four got out. They wore loose-fitting windbreakers in different colors.

They entered the store.

The Toyota showed empty.

"It's going down now," I sputtered.

My fingers punched in 911.

"San Risa County, 911," a different woman's voice said. "Where is the emergency?"

"23112 Main Street, Basta, at the Desert Market," I said. My voice waved up and down. "Four men, two Latino, two Anglo, just went inside. I think that they are going to do a robbery."

"Sir, did you call before?"

My mouth worked. It said foul words without making noise.

"Oh, damn the luck!" I managed to say.

"Excuse me, sir? What did you say?"

"Yes, I called before," I said. "But they are inside now."

She paused.

Someone spoke near her.

"Let me give you descriptions," I said.

"All right, sir," she said. "We'll send somebody."

The line died.

BAM!

It came from inside the Desert Market.

Three more BAM! BAM! BAM! came.

"I'm open!" I hissed.

My body was on the scrubby grass near the parking lot. They could shoot me without half trying.

The Desert Market front door lay 60 feet away.

Crutches and duffle bag tangled in my legs as I crutched away.

Dust choked me.

The drifters had already scuttled behind the trees when they heard the shots.

The combat veteran drifters flattened out. Their training kicked in.

I tried to roll behind the dumpster and lifted the shotgun towards the Desert Market. The duffle bag covered the shotgun. Nobody could see it. But I racked a round into the chamber.

Customers raced out of the Desert Market. Their bodies jerked to get away. Mouths gaped.

Some screamed.

The robbers scrambled out. They wore nylon stockings. The stockings smeared their faces. An assault rifle bobbed wildly. Another waved a shotgun.

They tore open the Toyota doors.

I could not shoot them. It was against the law for me to shoot. They were fleeing.

They filled the Toyota.

The Toyota rolled.

I let the shotgun down inside the duffle bag and took out the camera. My fingers shook. I shot three long-range pictures of the Toyota.

A woman wearing a gray Desert Market smock bobbed out of the door. Her glasses glinted. BAM! She dropped. A sawed-off shotgun waved out a Toyota window. The woman rolled on the ground. Blood smeared her smock.

Others exploded out of the doorway. They screamed. Cars shot past out of the parking lot. Californians fled trouble in their cars.

I dropped the camera.

My hands found the shotgun.

Cars blocked my view of the Toyota.

If I could not see my target, I could not shoot. Buckshot spread too far. It might kill an innocent.

A gray van cut the Toyota off and stopped. The driver was a woman wearing a baseball hat over her white curls. She did not look like a crime fighter. She sped up, away from the market.

Three more cars slopped past.

They did not seem to know about the robbery. This was just another day at the Desert Market.

A Basta police car slewed into the parking lot. Brakes squealed.

The cops gunned the engine toward the Desert Market doorway. That was bad tactics.

A sheriff's tan car flashed down Main Street. The blue roof light spun.

"Over here!" a drifter shouted. "Here!"

The deputy driving the car did not stop. He passed the Desert Market.

"Dumb cacknackers," the drifter said. "What do you expect?"

Another Basta Police car came from behind the Desert Market. The driver tapped his siren.

The woman driving the van hit the gas. The van bucked forward. The cops shouted at her.

The cops were following the van. It was the wrong car. The robbers were in the Toyota.

"Toyota!" I shouted. "Stop the Toyota! Not the van!"

"That's them right there!" a woman shouted.

The cop cars surrounded the van.

The Toyota driver backed up.

"You in the van!" a cop shouted over his car loudspeaker. "Stop the van!"

The Toyota driver moved behind the cops. He inched the Toyota away. He looked like he was grinning. Nobody could blame him.

"Them officers blew right past the bad guys," a deep scratchy voice said. "That Toyota looks like Crosswaite's car. I seen him driving that Toyota last year. And Crosswaite is mean enough to rob the market. He always said that he wanted to tear Basta apart."

I raised my head. But I could not see who was talking. He had given up the name of "Crosswaite."

"Now look at them jacking that poor granny from the van," a skinny Latino drifter said, puffing on his cigar. "And granny did not do anything."

"That's their specialty," Whiskers said. "Innocent bystanders."

"Watch the van doors!" a red-haired Basta cop shouted. "She could be a faker. Might have suspects hiding inside to shoot!"

"That's the only wise thing said so far all morning," I said.

"You!" the red-haired cop shouted at the woman. "Step out of the van!"

"You in the van!" his partner shouted. "Don't move!"

"Bit of conflict there," I muttered.

"Why should I get out?" the woman driving screeched at the cops. "I didn't do anything!"

"Yes, you did!"

"What did I do, stupid?" she came back.

"Ah, the days of uniform," I said.

"You don't get out of that van, I'll shoot you!" the red-head said.

"I doubt that's legal," I said.

Risking the shotgun, I let it lay and stepped towards the drifters.

"Did you say that the Toyota belongs to Crosswaite?" I asked them.

Nobody answered.

But I had to try.

"Come on, guys," I pleaded. "They shot a woman."

"Ain't gonna shoot me," the bald man with the red bandana said. "Crostwaite's smarter and tougher than those dumb laws."

"We don't talk to them laws," another said. His white whiskers exploded over a turkey-red face.

"They just roust us all the time," the man with the bandana said. "That's all they're good for."

The county sheriff's car swung into the parking lot. Another sheriff's car joined him. They drove to where the Basta cops were pulling the older woman driver out of her van.

The sheriff's deputies jumped out of their car. They saw that they had missed the action. So they drew their guns now.

"Holster that weapon!" a Basta sergeant shouted. "She's in our custody now!"

"It's county land!" the deputy said. "Not your jurisdiction. It is OUR territory."

"Since when?"

"Yeah, since when?" the woman driver asked from the ground. Her voice sounded muffled because her mouth was up against her left arm spread-eagled on the ground. She maintained the prone search position as a skinny Basta cop prodded her with a stainless steel shotgun.

"The back of the Desert Market is the dividing line!" the redhead shouted.

"It's the front of the Desert Market that's the boundary, you mullet-head!" another came back.

The drifters all melted away.

I put my camera down. My hands went inside the duffle bag. They worked the shotgun slide furiously.

Ten red shells went flying out of my hands and along the sand twenty feet away.

Then I rocked to my feet and kept my hands out of my pockets.

"Sheriff's Office!" a voice shouted behind me. "Freeze!"

I sighed.

"What's in that bag there?" the same voice said.

"Police officer," I said. I tried slowing down my voice. Or else, this deputy-type might panic and slaughter me. "Ex-New York cop. I'm the one who called you."

"Bag!"

"My camera. I filmed your suspects. And there's an empty shotgun in there. Mine."

"Why is it empty?"

"Because it's legal to have an empty one, Deputy. I just sat and watched and filmed the whole goat rodeo."

"What's a goat rodeo?"

"A mess."

He advanced, probably feeling stalwart. He frisked me with his free hand while the other held his black Beretta.

His round hard belly poked out in the tan uniform. Light brown head hair riffled in the breeze. Baby blue eyes rode above a cherub's full face. He looked like a laugher who enjoyed good beer and better food. If people were animals, he would be a roly-poly panda with his jolly face and eyes. But I was vexing him today and making him work.

"Deputy, shouldn't you please holster that as you search?"

"You trying to train me, slick?"

"Somebody should."

"You say you're an ex-police? And you're going to show and tell everything that went down today? That won't help nothing. The public will lose respect for us."

"They do not have it now."

"What's that smart remark? You with us or against us?"

"Do I have to choose?" I asked. "If I say nothing, you're going to keep rolling on an armed robbery in progress call the same way."

"It works okay," he said.

"If you keep doing it like that, cops and innocents will die for no reason," I said. "If I have to hurt your feelings to save lives, I will do it."

Chapter 8

Sheriffing, More Or Less

A bystander in the Del Taco fast-food joint guffawed. "I heard people say that one robber looked like that kid Crosswaite. It was the Coach Martiska said it. Even with a mask on, Crosswaite looked familiar to the coach."

"Crosswaite always did have a wild streak in him. Now I bet that he is running haywire around here."

My panda-looking deputy tilted the shotgun up to his nose and sniffed. His face relaxed.

"Why didn't you shoot at them?" he asked.

"Because they were fleeing and I'm a civilian. I can only shoot to protect a life. Or else I go to prison."

"Technically, you're right, I guess."

"Prison is very technical. My name's Max Royster."

"Enrique Mendoza," he said. His handshake crushed mine. "Dude, you got to cut me some slack about the frisk and all that."

"It's a hot call," I said. "They are always messy. Consider yourself cut some slack, Enrique."

His blue-eyed panda face relaxed into a smile. He smelled of vanilla, gun leather heated by the sun and his hair oil.

The county ambulance roared down Main Street with all the Christmas lights a-dancing on the roof and banshees wailing across the crisp desert air.

"What's with you deputies and the local Basta Police Department?" I asked.

He sighed.

"Part of Basta proper is theirs," he said. "Part is ours. Even the mayor isn't sure which is which. It's under review now. They're a good outfit. Hellfire, WE are a squared away group ourselves. This sheriff's office, this S.O., is usually squared away. It's just that some of our deputies in the Basta substation like to relax too much."

"I'm ex-NYPD, remember? We know all about relaxing too much."

"I've got to help on the crime scene here," Mendoza said.

"I'm part of it. Get me into your substation ASAP," I said.

"Why?"

Taking a notebook out of my back pocket, I flipped it open and started sketching a man's body.

"This is the one who shot the woman here," I said. "I'm doing this from memory now. There were three other bandits, right? I can have the other three sketches done in fifteen minutes and hand them to your boss."

"I don't know about that," Mendoza said. "Let me check with my supervisor."

"Oh, that word!" I said.

More patrol cars, both sheriff and police, clogged up the parking lot. Plainclothes deputies with stars on their sports shirts piled out of their unmarked cars. A boss with white hair showed that this was a serious call.

I lifted my camera out of the duffle bag again and snapped shots of the parking lot.

"Max, that's not authorized," Mendoza said. "You going to sell those to the media?"

"They'll be here soon enough," I said. "What I'm doing is getting pictures of the license plates for you. Lot is full of witnesses. Some will leave in the next ten minutes without speaking to you. Trace these plates and you can talk to them tonight about what they saw."

"You can give that to the detectives," he said.

"When cats bark. Some real working cop should interview these drivers today. Remember that memory fades amazingly after you sleep. You lose it overnight. I'm forty-six and my memory goes fast after a night's sleep. That's why I'm sketching now."

"The sheriff's detectives don't like us deputies messing in their cases."

"Any sheriff's detectives here now?" I asked.

He scanned the rolling, hurly-burly crowd and shook his panda's head.

"None that I can see," he said. "Goddamn it all to hell."

"And there probably won't be. At least, not for a while. Not if they are like some NYPD detectives. So working cops like you and I have to step up and get things done."

"Wait right here," he said.

I leaned my crutches against his cruiser and sketched some more.

Radio calls blared. The ambulance siren and did its best to distract me. But I kept sketching.

As an artist, I made a great bartender. But, in Patrol, I had learned some basics in witness reconstruction from the NYPD Sketch Unit. They had told us to emphasize any face feature that the witness remembered. Today, I was the witness, and I reached back for their lessons again.

"You the jerk wants a ride to the substation?" a new voice asked.

A sheriff's deputy with three sergeant's chevrons on his short sleeves strode over to my spot. His nameplate read "Gwynn."

Clear speech seemed necessary now.

He looked tricky.

"Sarge, I want to give my statement and turn over my film to you," I said. "Along with my sketches of the suspects."

"You better speak to the detectives about that," he said. "We can't be responsible, slick. That's on their butts."

"Sarge, it's not the Mona Lisa original. They are just four sketches of the suspects. Because I bet that the supermarket's video cameras were not turned on."

He shot me a look.

"How did you know that?" he asked.

"Because they seldom are. Not when you want them on. Chain stores want to save cash. So they tell some underling to hit the button when something bad happens. They usually forget. Or the deal goes down before the underling knows it."

He sighed. A pear-shaped man with a whispery voice made for conspiracy; he stood about seven inches under my six feet. But muscles bulged everywhere on him, from the tendons in his bull neck to the thick blacksmith arms. Maybe he had weightlifted his way into the Sheriff's Department.

"Well, I'm sure afraid that that's what happened today," he said. "You want a ride into the substation? I've got a busy crime scene here. We aren't a taxi service, slick."

"Or a charm school."

"Why don't you drive in yourself?" he asked.

"My last car was in Hong Kong, about sixteen years ago. I don't think that I could find it in time today."

"How the hell are you living in Basta without a car?"

"Happily."

"Like your little jokes, don't you?"

"Why little?"

"Mister-"

"Officer. Police Officer Max Royster, NYPD. I was working directly under the Police Commissioner when I left for health reasons."

That was true enough, as far as it went. The Commissioner had ordered me to his office so that he could shatter me in person.

"Got your badge on you?"

"Shield. We turn them back in when we resign."

He sighed. With him, everything was a project.

"It'll take some time. But I'll see about getting you someone to take you in."

He made me sound like a kindergarten student with the colic who needed to see the school nurse.

It did take some time.

After what seemed like the Old Testament in slow motion, Mendoza came back to his patrol unit. Sweat stained his tan uniform. I knew the signs. It was not the heat. It was boss stress.

"Let's go," he said.

His tone said that he wanted to say much more.

Pitching an idiot grin on my face, I slapped him on his sweaty back.

"And how is the good Sergeant Gwynn?" I asked.

"Just like you see it. He's fine as long as he's sure that nobody, absolutely nobody nowhere, will ever be able to tie his tail in a knot for anything. Then he's behind you a hundred percent."

We rode along Main Street. More traffic was coming into the Desert Market parking lot. That way, everyone could say that they were there on the big day of the robbery-shooting.

"Like I say, the S.O. is a good place to work," he said.

"Or play. Your deputies never exit their cars to talk to anyone."

"Sure, we got some knuckle-heads in our ranks. Find me the cop shop that doesn't. We'll both join."

"True. You from here, Mendoza?"

"Since I was eight. I was born in Spain. Basque, if you can believe it."

"Basque in the California desert?"

"You anti-Basque or something?"

"I wouldn't know where to begin."

He dodged around a double-parked horse wagon with a full load of cayuses inside.

"Since you're a European, you view Basta differently from others," I said.

"Stop it. I've got to eat, keep my wife and kids safe and clothed. Six years in the S.O. already. Fourteen more to go until the pension."

Now that he had told me, I could hear a lilt to his voice, indicating that English was his second language.

We pulled onto the same strip mall that I remembered entering with Koy and Snowball-the-Wonder-Dog.

"You might want to watch your frigging onions while you're inside here," Mendoza said. "A little birdie says that there are hidden video cameras everywhere in the substation."

I slung the duffle bag over my shoulder and rocked myself onto my crutches.

Mendoza went to the side door and punched in a code. The door clicked.

We entered. Three concrete cells greeted us. Drunks or crooks lolled on the floors. The stench came back to me from before.

"Smells just like a New York booking cell," I said. "Fragrant. I call it 'Eau de Perp'."

"Where's my helpful witness?" a deep voice said from the tiny office off to the side.

A black man, about sixty, wearing the tan uniform leaned back in his swivel chair. Horn-rimmed glasses rode loosely on his nose above a scraggly moustache. When he smiled, large perfectly white teeth enlivened his face. His body looked like a runner's, with no spare flesh anywhere. He did not sport the crew cut that deputies seemed to favor. His hair was longish and wavy, brushed back from the high forehead.

Behind the glasses, he took in my crutches and dusty clothes. His mouth smiled again.

"I'm that guy, Sarge," I said, seeing his chevrons on the sleeve.

"You look a little reduced, sir," he said. "Reduced circumstances, as it were. I'm Rufus Caulk, the Watch Commander on this shift."

"Max Royster," I said. "Ex-cop. NYPD."

"And you come bearing gifts, sir?"

"Sketches of these mutts," I said. My notebook went onto his desk. "Do you want me to sign them? I don't know your evidence procedures here."

"I ask myself," Sgt. Caulk said. "Should we take them? Where's the up side for us here? And the downside?"

"The up side is that you use them as wanted flyers," I said. "And somebody recognizes him and peaches on him to you."

"By 'peaches' you mean that somebody squeals on him, right?"

"That's as plain as the joint on a male moose," I said.

"Sign them and date them," Sgt. Caulk said. "They can fire me for that or something else, I guess."

"And I'd like a receipt for my camera, Sarge. There are pictures of the robbers."

"Can't you do that yourself and then bill the county?"

"Chain-of-custody procedure, Sarge. If you want to produce these photos as evidence in court, some whiffle-ball defense lawyer will dance a buck-and-wing, challenging them in a Wade hearing. He will proclaim from the rooftops that they had too many grubby cop digits handling the precious photos, from me all the way to court. He may raise the issue that someone, maybe the CIA, or some rogue element in our invisible government, slipped the defendants' pictures in here."

"So?"

"So the way to avoid that is, I give the camera to you, the Sheriff's Office. You have your own lab cats work their magic with them and maintain the chain-of-custody all the way to trial."

Sgt. Caulk nodded, took my camera and started looking for a receipt form. There was no central system. Like most cops, he kept a picture of the files in his head. Memory took care of everything.

"I've just been in Basta a bit," I said. "But it seems as if there's a gap between the deputies and the residents, the Bastas."

"Indeed?"

"And I was breakfasting with some showbiz types, artists, and I got an idea. Sarge, do you think that Hollywood or Broadway have some of the most creative and versatile minds in the country?"

"I don't know about the best minds in the country. And neither do you. We are po-lice, and we work with what we got. What is this idea of yours?"

After I told it to him, he squinted at me through those horn-rimmed glasses with something like horror on his face.

"You can't be serious," he said. "This work is not for a bunch of unknowns and amateurs. We have written tests, background checks, psychological testing, a six-month academy and we still got to fire deputies every month."

"Don't you think that job stress turns normal recruits into crazed, acting-out, psychotic deputies?"

"No." he replied.

"Think again. How long is it since you came through the academy and had to cut your way through years of learning and failing?"

"If these Showbizzers, as you call them, have all these great skills, I applaud them. Let them apply to become Reserve Deputies with us. They'll be screened, tested and trained by professionals in our Reserve Academy."

I shook my head. The lines in Caulk's face deepened.

"None of these Showbizzers will want to crank out push-ups in an academy or wear a uniform," I said.

"Then how serious can they be?"

"That's what I want to find out," I said. "And I could use some help from you. Which, judging by your look right now, I don't think that I'm going to get."

"Royster, this appears to me as a dangerous fantasy. Don't you know that if you form this group and just one of them breaks the law, you yourself can get busted and locked down with Bubba the sodomite home asleep when they break this law? It's called 'conspiracy' or 'acting in concert in a criminal enterprise'. Do you want that?"

"Not this week."

"And there's another, more practical reason to drop this childish idea," Caulk said. "To go up against criminals as any kind of cop, you need guns, respect and power. The early FBI tried to send agents into the field without any of that. They wound up burying some of those young agents after crooks laughed at them and blew them apart with Tommy guns. Families wept and fell apart. Are you prepared for that as well, Mister Big Talk?"

CHAPTER 9

What Happens When You Serenade?

Route 66 Arms greeted me when I got back home. I put my duffle bag and shotgun away.

The old sadness was starting again. That was no good.

Marcus and Koy were pounding down sodas on their front stoop. Moisture beaded the bottles. Marijuana smell flowered above them.

"No deputy units could bring me home," I said. "I had to dig into my inheritance for a cab. Charming way to treat a witness. No wonder normals avoid deputies here."

"Next time, call us," Koy said. "And pay us. Need the flipping money."

"Deputies rough you up or something?" Marcus asked.

Leaving out the part about my shotgun, I told them about the robbery. Koy looked wonderfully relaxed.

"You ARE a vigilante," Marcus said. He bounced up. "Koy, do you want another Doctor Pepper?"

"One was plenty, thanks. But what do you want? There's sweet talk coming again."

Marcus went inside.

This was going to be tricky. I sucked in a breath.

"Because of my crutches, I haven't really seen the desert," I said. "Could I ask you to drive me there with Snowball as chaperone for a poor man's picnic?"

She gazed at me. Her eyes were the color of coconuts against the cream of her eyes. Her slim face changed and lined a bit. Cheekbones rose in the heart-shaped face.

"Each idea you get is crazier than the next," she said. "What do you want?"

This was going to be a tougher sell than I had thought.

"But I am unable to get there on my own," I said.

"Yes, you can. It will just take you longer."

"And more pain. Today has been painful enough, thank you."

"Tell that to Snowball. I hate that desert."

"Lady Koy, there has been more than enough ugliness today. It is time for some beauty."

"So you get the idea to pitch me in the sand with the scorpions?" she asked. "Without asking me. Something that YOU decided. I am busy today. Wish that you'd find some other place to live."

Her voice rose a bit on this last part.

She whipped herself around and went inside the doorway of the house.

"Our hero has few options now," I muttered. The syrup of tiredness oozed back to me.

☙

My room did not look that attractive now. It never had, but now it looked worse.

My body eased down onto the squishy mattress. Back in Manhattan, I often slept on my floor with blankets in the winter. Crutches made that much tougher.

Affairs appeared to be in poor shape at the moment. There was no cash coming in from anywhere. On crutches in a desert town with only a temporary ID, no friends, and three thousand miles from home. All of this made me sigh.

"Our Hero must take heroic action," I said.

My voice echoed in this forgettable room.

The crutches dug into my armpits. The sweats came back.

Then I found myself in front of the Showbizzers house and taking a deep breath.

I sang as loudly as I could, to kill the tremors:

> Dark is the color of my true love's hair,
> Her cheek just like the lily fair!

"Who's that singing?" a man's voice shouted.

Marcus's head popped up in a window.

"It's not me!" he said. "I get paid for it. No more free showcases."

I plowed on with the song.

Above me, Snowball started barking.

Chick, our concierge, came to the back door of his office, looked at me and went back inside.

Snowball wailed.

"Now you woke him up!" Koy shouted.

Snowball's wet pink tongue wagged. He strengthened her mad.

He barked some more. He competed with me. It was a new game for him. Maybe he did not know crutches were for. Great Pyrenees dogs did not generally employ them.

Tensing my thigh muscles until they cramped, I forced myself to keep singing. The song was fast running out of lyrics.

It was time for a switch.

The first song was an old Scots ballad. It seemed wise to stay in the highlands of Scotland for the next song.

So the words came out:

> 'twas in the merry month of May,
> When greenbuds all were swelling,
> Sweet William on his death-bed lay
> For love of Barbara Allen.

From upstairs, someone played bagpipe music. It formed a Scottish background. Somebody was helping me with the mood. Maybe it was Zygolt doing this for me. If so, good. She seemed to be the top-kick boss of the Showbizzers. They would follow her lead.

Or maybe she was laughing at me. Maybe everyone else was.

"A cheap way to get my attention," Koy said.

That demanded an answer.

"Why do you say that?" I asked. "It's the purest form of showbiz. And we are all Showbizzers now. You when you train Snowball, Zygolt when she stretches, Marcus when he rehearses his lines. I'm just becoming one of you now."

She made a face, fumed and stepped away from the window.

Snowball bloomed white and fluffy and bounding joyously through the doorway. His muzzle formed a wonder of wet. White canines flashed.

Koy appeared behind him. Her slim face tightened and she waved her hands at me.

"Okay! All right!" she hooted. "You woke him from his nap! So I must as well take both you animals out for your walk. Why am I even thinking about doing this?"

"Because I'll pay for your gas."

"Yes?"

"Romantic, isn't it?"

"Craparoo. Another man myth. Tell it to Snowball."

"Snowball can be our chaperone," I said. "He has the proper dignified look to control animal appetites."

❧

She drove the Jeep rapidly but skillfully.

"What do you feel like eating?" I asked Koy.

She did not answer.

Maybe she was one of those who did not speak while driving.

Or maybe the words that could come out might depress me.

We flashed past the square in Old Town. The fringes of desert homeless were starting to form. They would be talking up the Desert Market robbery all night.

A shrewd detective should be with the crowd tonight, buying Bourbon shots to loosen tongues. My mentor and hook, Al Lipkin, would be on the crowd's edge, appearing to sleep when necessary and to smile encouragingly when called for.

But I was in this Jeep, alongside warm and shaggy Snowball, pitching woo to his mistress.

Pastel blue and tungsten colors lit up the sky overhead.

"When I was a kid in New York City," I said, scratching to set a mood. "The cowboy movies always showed a lovely and dynamic blood-red sunset against puffy white clouds and a pale blue sky. I thought that those sunsets were all Hollywood necromancy and fakery. But now I see that those sunsets were real. They happen every day."

She still stayed dumb.

"Is there some reason why you're holding your mud?" I asked.

"Excuse me?"

"That's an improvement. Did you know that Abraham Lincoln called the West 'the Treasure Chest of this Nation'?"

"He never saw it."

"Well, maybe someone sent him a picture postcard."

"Huh!"

"Could you stop at this service station, please?" I asked. "I need something to wash down my medicine with."

"Royster," she said. I did not think that she had remembered my last name. "Anyone ever tell you that you need special care?"

The Chinese accent flavored her words again.

She whipped the Jeep onto a Circle K store with gas pumps and newspaper racks outside.

My crutches rolled me into the store. They did not sell much food that an adult would want to choke down. But I took another deep breath and tried to think romantically.

She was stroking Snowball's neck when I returned.

"Did you buy the store?" she asked.

We broke out of strip mall territory. The scrubby grass thinned and then seemed to go into the golden earth.

A range of mountains, purple just like the song said, appeared far to our right. Fading sunlight etched black lips against the surface.

Koy put the Jeep onto a dirt road, rode it a hundred yards and then stopped it.

Snowball yelped and bounded from the Jeep. His tail twitched madly. I felt pretty much the same way. The landscape was working its magic on me.

"That's what you bought?" Koy asked as I opened the purple plastic shopping bag with. "Circle K – Shop With Us Again" stamped on it. "Beef jerky, Almond Joy bars and Fresca?"

"They were fresh out of *Canard à l'Orange.*"

I was trying for the right touch.

"Do you think that Fresca is romantic?"

"It was either that or Valvoline Motor Oil. They had a lot of that on sale."

Settling painfully on the scrabby sand, I concentrated on the sunlight still walking across the mountains.

"Do they have a name?" I asked.

"Locals call them the Calico Mountains. Way full of silver deposits."

"This is very good of you, Koy."

"Better thank Snowball. He talked me into it. And you haven't paid me for the gas yet."

My left knee still throbbed. The Fresca did nothing to quell it.

Her eyes shuttered and then looked at Snowball. It was a look that I had seen before on other people.

"Koy, what's wrong?"

"Nothing."

"That's a bit too quick."

"What are you asking?" she said. "What do you want?"

"Nobody ever called me insensitive. Some people are rocks, some are tuning forks. There are many things that I can never learn to do. But I can sense trouble."

"You're making something out of nothing," she said.

"Tell me about this nothing."

We both watched Snowball frolic some more. The fresh dry desert grass smell came back to me.

"Awful, awful, awful. Maybe I'm awful company today," she said.

"I'm not too sparkling myself. Armed robberies tend to dent the day's joy."

"Well, I'm going for some tests pretty soon and cancer runs in my family, if that's the medical term for a tendency towards it. Mother and aunts and uncles go through chemotherapy, some not making it. Cancer sucks."

"No argument."

"And us Chinese families, we supposed to get it less often than you round-eyes. Diet is usually healthier."

"All that fish," I said.

"As a freelancer, I gotta fork up for my own health insurance. And the rates blast up higher than high. Every time a politician on TV shoots off his mouth about healthcare, I get scared again. I won't be able to pay my bill, and they'll throw me out of the clinic because of it. Scared, that's the word for sure. You betcha."

"What do the other Showbizzers say about this?"

"Stop calling us that. We're very individual people, you know. When you call us that, you're like some horrid dark Pied Piper of the underworld trying to drag us down with you."

"Your housemates, then. What do they say?"

"We kids pay for our own health insurance. So we like take dumb craparoo jobs that make us ashamed but have health benefits stuck on them like a sign. That sign says 'I can't make it on my own'. I mean, really."

"And I worry, worry all the time that I may have to sell Snowball to pay for my damn treatments. He is the best dog that I ever trained. Like my big brother."

"I could be his substitute," I said. "We're both big and hairy."

"You're too old for me."

She wrapped her arms around her knees, hugging herself.

"And your whacko ideas about us playing policeman can get us all killed. Do you really think that will work or are you talking big to show off for us kids?"

"I believe it," I said truthfully. "No Bolshoi."

"This does not interest me. Why are you trying to get us to do your bidding in this craparoo?" she asked. "And who will pay us? What kind of fool works for free?"

"You're trying to hammer out an artist's colony in a desert town, Koy. Before you can perform, you have to be safe."

"Bull. Look at the productions that come out of Los Angeles every year. Is Los Angeles safe? Is Vegas? Or New York?"

"You'll be giving back to the community."

"Spare me," she said. She was getting too close to where I lived. "I donated my life to Animal Rescue for years as a volunteer. Took forever to learn my trade. I gave back plenty already. What's the real reason?"

"Would you like some beef jerky?"

"I don't eat meat," she said.

"You think that I'm just another Southern California big talker fraud, with four cellphones, a wife and kids hidden somewhere and a lot of meaningless words."

I sighed and looked at the Calico Mountains.

"I always hated bullies," I said. "They scared me, too. On the ship, in kitchens, working as editors. I decided to do something to hit back against bullies, so I pounded down some whiskeys with my buddies, talked big, as you said. The next morning, hung over, I took the test for the cops."

Her coconut eyes scrutinized me again.

"And you became a policeman?" she asked.

"NYPD. Seven-One Precinct, Brooklyn."

"Why aren't you working now?"

"Medical reasons."

"Like mine?" she asked. "Stop playing around with me, with all of us. You come into here, Basta, and you try pumping us up with this off-the-wall idea."

"It's not off-the-wall," I said. "You artists keep saying that, in your art, you have the sharpest and most creative minds in America. All I'm asking is that you set up communications between yourselves and sworn deputies and let them benefit from all that wit. I'm saying to outthink the crooks, not to try kicking switchblades out of their hands."

"It sounds like a fantasy to all of us."

"Koy, I'm not somebody big or important, and I never will be. Divorced, no kids. No family that needs me. The younger cops ignored my tips on how to work. I was never able to change much in policing. Here in Basta, of all places, I get a late chance to make a difference. Showbizzers, let's crush crime."

"With us as your guinea-pig?"

"Nothing much changes in police work, in the blue parade. This small idea could make big changes."

"And then you don't tell us your real story," she said.

"Nobody asked."

"Because we didn't want up to wind up like you."

"It's not summer at the beach, I grant you," I said. "You're the only one I told. Please tell the others."

"Damn right I will. I'll warn them that you're obsessed with fighting crime."

"Actually," I said. "I was obsessed with getting paid every two weeks."

"You want to use our brains and bodies to get back what you lost. I was right. You are some kind of evil guide to hell."

"Koy, I can't recover what I lost. The Department fired me for depression. I'm trying to get some medical benefits and they are hoping that I just give up trying or go and die somewhere."

"Let's go," she said. Her voice shook. "Pick up your ridiculous food. If you come near me now, I'll have Snowball tear you apart. He'll do whatever I tell him."

"So will I."

"Now that I know that you're a crazy ex-cop, I'm just way scared of you. That's all. And you still didn't pay for the gas."

Chapter 10

Learning

The next morning, before breakfast, someone rapped on my door. There was nothing for me to protect anymore. I opened the door.

"I think that you're right," Clytemnestra said.

"Of course I am," I said. "About what?"

"This wiggy idea of yours," she said.

Her blue eyes gleamed in the narrow face under the explosion of red hair. She was wearing a lime green jogging outfit and red Puma running shoes and looked like a woman warrior exhilarated with the battle of life.

The sun was just coming up. I could smell it start to heat the scrabby grass around my room. Clytemnestra's perfume blended with it.

"You're wearing fresh perfume?" I asked. "For running in the morning."

"Never know who you might meet."

"You are a Showbizzer, all right."

"I want to try your idea," she said. "It's kicks to get out there and put it all on the line. It's just like, here I am, and do whatever you want. Koy says that you used to be a cop. Isn't that how you felt?"

"Maybe after doughnuts."

"The others don't know yet. They are up in Big Bear Lake with some friends. What I want to do is cruise the bars like Shooters, Hooz-on-First and the Idle Spurs Steak House, leave tips, make friends and listen to what I hear."

"That's exactly right," I said. "But how did you know to do that? Most people wouldn't."

"After tending bar in the Purple Jester in Mishawaka, Indiana, you realize that everything in the world comes out in your local saloon if you just wait long enough."

"Words to live by. But you're the only young redhead that I've seen in Basta. You have to make sure that none of these barfly types can find out where you live. If someone just sees your red hair going into these Route 66 cabins, your safety is compromised."

"Life is full of risks."

"Yes. And if you're wise, you avoid them. Don't think that this is a dress rehearsal. These waddies will drive a railroad spike through your left eye, go wash down nine burritos with beer and sleep for twelve hours without thinking about you."

"That's exciting."

"Not to most people," I said. "When do you want to start this?"

"Tonight."

"Whoa," I said. "Let's think about that."

"Or maybe this afternoon. If we wait too long, they'll find something else to gossip about. It won't be the hot topic that we want it to be."

"You're right again. Okay. Showbizzers, break a leg and crush crime. How's your drinking?"

"Oh, I love to drink. Bacardi rum, straight. And to smoke, tobacco or grass. And to make love with anyone who turns me on."

"I won't ask about hard drugs. I'm scared to."

"I'm not," she said.

"But I do want you to listen for the name of 'Crosswaite'," I said. "His name came up as a suspect during the robbery. If you can, get people talking about Crosswaite."

"Got it," she said. "Crosswaite."

In the Showbizzer house, someone was playing soft classical guitar. Maybe it was Snowball. It blended with the crows cawing as they drifted on thermals overhead.

"Some background rules, Clytemnestra. Is that your real name?"

"My parents were hippies."

"When the children of hippies show lines in their faces, then I know that I am getting older." I said. "Please take only cash. No ID. Nothing with your name on it. Wear your hair in a style that you never wear it in. Use that style only when you go to these bars. Leave your phone here. If you please, take off your rings, wristwatch or jewelry. They can identify you later on, if your subject has a good memory. Remember that bars have video cameras everywhere."

"This is going to be fun."

"What's the name of your first boyfriend?" I asked.

"There were quite a number of them."

"All at the same time? Use one name, if you can remember him. This morning, start writing a letter to him. Yes, on paper. Like our grandparents did. Fill it with just chat about anything. When you three paragraphs done, fold it and put it in your pocket. Add two reliable pens."

"Why am I doing all this?"

"Because you may not hear anything worthwhile tonight. But if you do, you'll need to write it down. Go to the bathroom, sit in the stall and lock this door."

"Quite detailed, Max."

"I'm laughing, too. Write down what the person said. Hide it inside that letter that you already started. Make up your own code if you have to. Then, as soon as you get home, write out everything that you saw and heard that pertains to that stuff you put in the letter. Everything. Hat sizes. The night vision of the wild dingo dog. Sign it and date it. Keep both the pieces of paper under lock and key until you need them."

"Why, my god, why?"

"Because if this ever goes to court, you will want to turn both papers over to the prosecution. The D. A. can use it to strengthen the case."

She shook her classic head with the full head of hair.

"Max, I'm not any kind of cop. Nobody will care what I wrote down."

"Yes, they will. Trust me. I've been there."

"All right. Now I'm going for my shower. Koy and I are going to the Firehouse Restaurant for breakfast. She asked me to come alone."

"That is a kind of code," I said. "That means that she's had enough of me. Many people agree with her."

"I don't like leaving you here without wheels."

"I'll chew on a bullet."

After she left, I folded myself back down onto my mattress. My knee ached. It kept me awake for a while.

Then I drifted back into delicious sleep. The room heated up as the sun climbed higher.

§

Knocks sounded on my door again. I hobbled closer to it.

Police radio calls sounded from the other side. Maybe Clytemnestra had gotten too enthusiastic and swiped a cop radio.

Enrique Mendoza stood outside in his tan uniform. The six-point deputy's star shone on his left breast pocket. The radio was gurgling like mad.

"Can't stay long," he said, baby blue eyes darting around. "Gila Bank opened up this morning. About a dozen customers came in. So did three knuckleheads with masks, sawed-off shotguns and assault rifles. One jumped on top of the counter and put everyone on the floor. The guard is unarmed, sixty-four years old and reads Scripture in the Basta Baptist Church."

"Useful in the next world but not in this one," I said.

"Suspect Number One, on the counter, waves a pump-action sawed-off from a shoulder sling," Mendoza said. "He keeps everyone's face to the floor."

"Suspect Two spray-paints the robbery cameras. He's got an AK-47 on a sling, ammo vest and probably body armor because the wits say that he seemed bulky. Around his back, he's got a sawed-off double-barreled shotgun, just in case. Nobody wants to mess with him, gunned up like that. Two .45s on his waist."

"This is a serious man," I said.

"You might say that. Suspect Number Three has his AK-47 from the corner of the bank. That way, nobody can get behind him."

"One of the lady tellers, Michelle Ashcroft, had been working there since they rolled back the rock on Jesus. And she's been robbed four times before. Nobody can figure out why but today she made a move and hit the silent alarm button on the floor near her cage. Suspect Number One, Counterman, saw her move. 'You did that for the bank's money?' he asked. Nobody knew what he was talking about. Michelle knew. She started to edge away.

"'No, I didn't –' was as far as she got. Counterman aimed and blew a buckshot charge into her face. She ain't got no face now. Her eyeglass frames blew apart along with her. Wits found parts of both on their clothes and in their hair. One customer had part of her face lodged inside his earlobe."

"All for cash," I said.

"Our headshrinker, the bug doc, says that armed robbers get high off the rush of taking down a score. They could make more and safer bread by fraud."

"Like computer repair."

"So, with Michelle all graveyard dead, Suspect Number Two got the manager to open the vault. Or else, he said, he would start executing customers."

"That's rare stuff," I said. "Most bank robbers don't go that violent anymore. Most just go for note jobs, no gun seen, and get sixteen hundred on the average."

"With his head teller dead, I don't blame him for opening the vault," Mendoza said. "We got the alarm at our substation. We get false alarms all the time."

"I remember mine," I said.

"Goddamn county only gives us three units in the Basta area. 'Let the Basta town po-lice handle their own messes', they say."

"That really helps the citizens," I said.

"That AK-47 makes a noise that you never forget. Desert riff-raff fella begging money outside the bank hears it. He's begging nickels and dimes, but he got six years in the Army and a working cellphone."

"The team scoops up about twenty-seven thousand from the vault and cages. Nobody of the victims is moving after Michelle got exploded. Counterman has an earphone in. Maybe listening to our fricking radio channel. He keeps shouting out minutes and seconds like he's a goddamned track coach. One taxpayer inside the bank, on the floor, has a 9mm Browning in a pancake holster under his shirt. He has to make a quick decision. He makes the right one. Leave the gun in the holster or wind up like Michelle there on the floor. Like you say, it is only money."

"Did I say that?"

"Basta cops get the call from the riff-raff. They start rolling. Then Michelle's hold-up button alarm comes through. Now they realize that it's real beer. The first unit gets to the mall parking lot. Counterman is still up on his counter. Cop is unlocking his shotgun from the unit's front mount. But the cop messes up. Like most of us would, he wants to get in close. Where the action is. His unit parks in line of sight from the bad guys. He does not angle his car away from them for protection, the way they teach us in the county academy. He just parks dead in front like it's a false alarm. But he knows that it is not.

"Number Three is there to remind him. He has got his AK-47 pointed out past the bank's plate-glass window. As soon as he sees that shotgun get loose, he shoots through the window. It's just glass. Banks don't armor themselves or anything like that. The AK is a real man-stopper, even at long range. Just ask Al-Qaeda. Those 7.62 rounds chew up the cop's car. He ducks down under the dash. The engine block saved his life. He's lucky that he's not breathing dirt right now.

"He's digging down deep in that car. No shotgun in play. Another unit is rolling into the lot. Counterman has got Suspect Number Two finished with the cash grab. Now Counterman gets his bright fricking idea. I never heard of one like this.

'Everyone up and out that door!' Counterman shouts out. 'Do it now! Anyone on the floor, I'll kill them. GO!'"

"A local citizen, Johnny Detweiler, is in the parking lot and hears the shots. He's near his pickup truck and yanks out his 30-30 lever action Winchester. You New York liberals always joke about us carrying guns in our trucks. This time, it helped.

"Old Det puts five rounds downrange at Suspect Two as he comes out the doorway. Something hit him. Wits saw him stagger. But he's got that vest on. So he goes down but gets back up again. The second unit has got a clear shot at Suspect Number Two. He does not take it. Innocent bystanders in the way, he says now. Well, maybe they were. But we can't find them. Neither did nobody else see them."

"For most people, even cops, it's hard to shoot another person," I said. "Civilization kicks in."

"Whatever. By now, the victims are up and running out that door to safety. They think. Now the front of the bank is so crowded with bystanders and tellers that the cops do not have clear targets. It is a mess. Just like Counterman wanted. No copper is going to put rounds downrange into that crowd. If someone dies, that cop will wind up in prison hisself."

"Or feel remorse forever," I said. "And put his own check back in the rack."

"Huh?"

"Suicide," I said. "Doing-the-Honorable-Thing."

"Suspect Two sees Detweiler behind his truck and lets loose another magazine. Bullets chew up the truck. Det is already running from the pickup, trying to reload. The first cop to arrive shoots his shotgun. But he's too far away to hit them. A police shotgun is for closer work. The spread scattered.

"Suspect Number Three goes through the door and takes up a position behind a pillar. He shoots at both cop cars. Their time is running out now. Any more cop cars show now, these suspects got real problems.

"The other two are already getting into a blue Oldsmobile parked behind a parked van. That van blocks the coppers' line of sight. Counterman is like the commanding officer, last one to leave. Disciplined. Maybe ex-military. He's running and firing that AK. Bullets everywhere. Shotgun hits the Oldsmobile. But it keeps moving. Counterman jumps inside. Detweiler has reloaded and puts more rounds through the car's windows. But did you ever try to stop an all-steel car with just bullets?"

"Yes," I answered. "It does not work."

"The Oldsmobile takes a licking but it keeps on ticking. It makes it through the parking lot and out into Main Street. The windows were shot out, but that engine is powerful. That's why they picked it. One of our deputy units thinks that he passed it, going in to handle the alarm."

"Hate to say it," I said. "But your deputy units are good at passing by real suspects."

"Yeah, I know. Like the supermarket caper. Don't tell nobody, I mean nobody, that I gave you any of this info. Sgt. Caulk will have me directing traffic in an alley."

"Are you headed to the bank now?"

"Yeah."

"Give me a lift there?"

Mendoza's blue eyes clouded for once.

"If someone sees you, it's my butt," he said. "You don't know how our Sheriff is about civil liability. He screams at us about not putting outsiders in our cars unless there is a clear police reason for it. You know?"

"I know," I said. "That's why I'm freelance."

Chapter 11 All That Mess

Fry Me Up A Mess

After Mendoza left, I scrabbled through my clothes for something that a serious professional might wear. A black short-sleeve work shirt and black jeans seemed the best choice. My old black soft-soled patrol shoes completed the look.

"That's me," I said to my tiny mirror on the cracked wall. "A committed criminal justice professional."

Some cops mistrusted anyone with glasses. They saw them as being weaker than the policeman herd. So I switched from my jolly green glasses to soft contact lenses.

"The Police Commissioner tried to commit me himself," I said.

Digging down into my retirement fund, I called High Desert Cab and gave my address.

They dispatched a freckled chatterbox in his sixties who kept calling me "Cowboy" and told me what he had heard about the bank robbery and murder.

He listened when I mentioned that I was trying to find an old buddy of mine named Crosswaite around Basta. I had to start somewhere. He said that he had heard the name before but that was all. His company card fit into my hand. It might come in handy later.

The Gila Bank was set inside another of Basta's strip malls off Main Street. It shared space with a yoghurt store, Burger King and a few stores scattered under the adobe design. Today, about six Basta Police Department cars, painted in the old-fashioned black-and-white style, slanted throughout the parking lot. The blue uniforms of the Basta cops roved around the bank. Their shields were flat silver ovals, pinned to their left breast pockets. They looked like LAPD badges. The deputies wore silver six-pointed stars. Some cops were still on their hands and knees, trying to see any evidence that the earlier shift had missed. Shell casings littered the bank's front entrance. Plastic markers with numbers on them, about three inches long, lay next to the casings. Photographers with gold badges bent over and took shots.

None of the blue suits were talking with the tan uniforms of the deputies. To a New Yorker, that made a bad sign. The cops and the deputies sweated and ran patrol for different agencies but they should be talking to each other at a scene like this.

Sgt. Caulk leaned against a Sheriff's Department car, taking notes. His eyes fell on me and then looked away.

He was probably wishing that he had never opened his cubbyhole office door to me.

A statuesque black woman came out of the bank's front door. She ducked under the yellow crime scene by lifting it up and sliding underneath it.

She wore a pants suit the color of her skin and a light blue frilly dress shirt. Her shoes were flats, with rubber soles. Her hands were large and square with no rings anywhere. She looked to be in her mid-thirties. Her hair was cut short and drew attention to her strong face. The pants suit jacket humped a bit over her right hip. She looked like an FBI agent to me.

It was a cinch that she was not going to approach me. So I crutches towards her.

"Excuse me," I said. "SA from the Bureau?"

"SA" stood for "Special Agent." Outsiders did not know the term. Jokers in the underworld like me would sling it around.

"Yessir," she said. "SA Merilee Combs, Basta Resident Agency. And you are?"

"Max Royster, ex-NYPD. I worked a kidnap with your Deputy Assistant Director Chichack."

"He just retired," she said. "And many baby agents are glad that he did. What can I do for you?"

"There's a lad named Crosswaite from here," I said. "No first name. The locals will have a jacket on him and all his info. There's loose talk, nothing for court, that he planned the Desert Market heist last week. This could be his catch-of-the-week."

She scribbled in a notebook and took my information as well.

"I know that you're busy right now, so I'll just drift," I said.

"What brings you to Basta?"

"January weather in New York on crutches."

"I hear that," she said. "What are you planning to do in Basta?"

The good gray FBI was not yet ready for my Showbizzer idea.

"Walk," I said. "Without crutches. I am a man of modest ambitions."

"And you picked me right out of this crowd as being Bureau?" she said. "How did you know that I wasn't a plain-clothes deputy or maybe corporate bank security?"

"On Patrol, I watched everyone for a living. To keep on living."

"And there aren't many black women in the local law," she said. "Not many blacks living out here in the first place. This country is way too dried up for my own taste. Give me Tampa. Have you been to the desert much?"

"Just for a picnic."

"Thanks for your help, Mr. Royster. If you hear anything else, here is my card."

She handed me a card with the royal blue and gold FBI seal.

More sheriff's cars came in.

Thanking Special Agent Combs, I stepped away from the FBI, button-hooked on my crutches and came back to the bank's front.

Then I went around the back. There were no uniforms there and no yellow crime scene tape. But there might be some trace evidence. Someone could have dropped something in their flight. The wind could have moved it around to the back. Nobody was likely to tell me now what direction they had fled in. The official lid on information was shut tight.

For the next half hour or so, I leaned on my crutches there and visualized the scene.

The site was a smart one for a robbery crew. The bank was just a five minute drive to the big Freeway, 15. It ran east or west from here. Three minutes east of here, you could exit 15 onto Highway 40. That also ran to the east or west.

The law would need at least four cars to block freeway entrances and lock down the robbers. And the crew could just flee down Main Street or into the desert where Koy had taken me.

There were no clues that jumped out at me. I kept going over in my head where I would go after pulling this score. Not knowing the territory first hand was a real problem. Maps would come in handy later.

Making my way back to the front, I saw the police and deputy crowd had gotten bigger.

The crowd of onlookers was growing fast, too. Some faces I memorized and some I took sketched, without them noticing. Then my pen took down the different license plates. Later, I could start up a file of face shots in my room. Maybe I could match them to names or license plates later.

Another marked Sheriff's car came from Main Street. It cut sharp inside, braked and a tall hardpacked man in the tan uniform got out. He was hawk-faced and aggressively good-looking, with straight black hair and heavy charcoal brows over an outdoorsman's face. His Sam Browne gunbelt gleamed next to the holstered Beretta gun.

Six hash stripes rode on his left forearm. That meant thirty years of deputy service.

"Here's the sheriff right now," a younger deputy said from the group in front. "He's not looking too happy."

I could imagine why. Popular votes elected or defeated the candidates for sheriff. If the voters thought that he could not do anything to stop robberies and murders, he would soon be in ex-sheriff limbo

To a New Yorker like me, the idea of voting your top cop into office made me smile. It seemed like a holdover from the Old Western days where they carried the law in a holster.

A couple of sergeants crowded near the sheriff, but he waved them away with his hand. They turned their boots away from him and let him pace into the bank alone. The Basta cop holding up the crime scene tape and keeping a clipboard of people who entered and left did not speak to the sheriff. He just jotted something down on the clipboard and let the sheriff enter.

The sheriff's star had the words stamped on it, "Sheriff, San Risa County."

The California state seal lay enameled in the star's center.

His nametag read Nelson.

It was my time to try doing something for humanity. Stage-fright chilled me for a minute. Then I approached the sheriff.

"Excuse me, Sheriff Nelson," I said. "May I speak with you for a minute?"

He stopped six feet from me.

"Good afternoon, sir," he said, eying my crutches.

Maybe he thought that I was some wounded war veteran, worthy of respect.

"Have we met?"

"Nossir. I'm an ex-cop from New York and I've got an idea to make your life easier and your town safer."

He stopped and gave me a busy-man look.

This was my shot. I gave him the Showbizzer concept.

"Interesting idea," he said. "But I'm pretty darn busy right now. This isn't the time or the place for a talk. Nice meeting you."

The political machine that was Sheriff Nelson rolled past me without a look back. He did not offer me a good-bye hand-shake. He was probably concerned with where my right hand might have been picking up airborne pathogens and other un-happy illnesses.

He went and conferred with three men in jackets and bolo ties. Star badges winked on their belts.

"Get over here, Royster," Caulk said. "Are you some kind of demented prophet crying out in the desert?"

"Now that you mention it-"

I could not tell what Caulk was feeling. Those eyes hid his emotions behind the tortoise-shell frames. Other lawmen acted like that. They had seen emotions run amuck and set baby girl children on fire. He had seen rookie deputies get emotional over hookers, fall in love with one and blow out his brains in front of his parents and wife.

Emotions were something that Caulk would run from.

"What did you hope to accomplish?" Caulk asked.

"My only job skill is annoying adults."

"I'm starting to see that. He's going to be upset that my shift let someone like you get that close to him."

"Then he should stay out of politics," I said. "There's no law stopping me from talking to a public official. Was this Crosswaite and his team hitting the bank today?"

"We don't know who it was," Caulk said. "That's the word so far. Royster, I have to put up with *The Desert Dispatch* and the rest of the media and pretend that they know what they are doing when they drag my department's name through the mud. But I don't have to put up with you and your New York City crackpot ideas."

"Don't blame my ideas on New York, Sarge," I said. "They are strictly my own."

"I can believe that," he snapped. "Why don't you head back home, Royster? You stay around here, getting involved in one mess or another, and you'll wind up in the joint. When the other inmates learn that you're an ex-cop, they will punish you for it."

"In the showers," I said. "Where I'll learn a lot about manly love. Thanks for the word, Sergeant."

"You better remember it."

"I'll have trouble forgetting it."

Mendoza looked like he wanted to hurl something at me.

There was nothing more for me to mess up here at the scene. Like a gambler going into a game with just five bucks, when I broke even, it was time to push away from the table.

Funds were getting tighter. So I got the crutches going and wheeled my way towards the Route 66 Arms.

❧

The trip gave me time to think.

The noonday sun tightened. My professional outfit was getting quite wet with sweat.

Whenever I try impersonating a professional, I step on my own face.

Cars barreled past me.

I tried to look noticeable. The Showbizzers might be coming back from their trip.

Finally, the Router 66 Arms loomed up ahead.

With my arms twitching from the strain, I hauled my own freight into my own room and onto my bed. Lying there, I rolled out of my outfit and into T-shirts and cut-offs.

The Buick Roadmaster that the Showbizzers used every day lay parked in front of their house. Their home had private bathrooms. But I had to share a shower and bath with other guests. So the Showbizzers were back by now.

The cold shower felt crisp against my hot skin. I cooled the hot pipes of my body and leaned against the wall of our common shower stall.

"It's time for a PowerPoint presentation, Foxy Maxy," I said. "This can't wait for tomorrow."

The towel rasped my skin.

The hummus supply had just one can left. I wedged into the cut-offs and T-shirt, jammed the can into my back pocket and made my slow way to the Showbizzer door.

༜

I knocked and Clytemnestra opened it. Zygolt, Marcus and Koy were sitting in the living room. Zygolt was playing with something in her hands. Snowball lay sideways on the floor. His big belly covered most of a throw rug.

The house smelled of sandalwood incense and laundry soap.

"'Lo, Max," Zygolt said.

That was a kind of acceptance.

"How was Big Bear Lake?" I asked. "I've heard about it from Roy Rogers but never been there."

"Who's Roy Rogers?" Koy asked.

"I forgot again. Wrong generation. He was a cowboy who lived at Big Bear."

"Cool heaven," Marcus said. "Lush and green. Not like this damn sorry sand around here."

"There's something that I wanted to mention," I said, setting out. My voice cracked a bit. Emotion made it crack sometimes. "Clytemnestra and Koy already know. I didn't think it worth mentioning before."

"Huh?"

"Like I said to some of you, I hate bullies," I said. "So I wanted to do something concrete about it. In New York, I kind of fell into the Police Department."

"That's a groovy trick," Zygolt said. "You were a cop?"

She held up the thing in her hands.

"You recognize this?" she asked. "It's a joint. Marijuana. You going to bust me, Officer?"

Her speech slurred. She had probably been smoking some already.

"That's an arrest that I never made," I said. "Never would make, either. I arrested men for beating their wives. Scalding their children to teach them manners."

"So now you have a nice fat pension?" Zygolt said.

Some women liked the idea of steady pension money rolling in every month. It was genetic, like childbearing.

"I got a bowl of steam," I said. "I served less than three chaotic years. Suspensions, days off, Notices-to -Correct, Restricted Duty. They do not pay me a penny."

"That's why you want us to be your little police robots," Marcus said. He looked high, too. "You want us to do what you couldn't do. That's Freudian!"

"No," Clytemnestra murmured. "More like Transactional Analysis."

"You guys enjoying this?" I asked.

"Be happy that we are," Koy said. "I'm off it because of my operation coming up. But I can drink this vodka all right."

"I have fallen in among hard-core party animals," I said.

"Damn betcha," Zygolt said. "And loving it."

"That same gang robbed the Gila Bank today," I said, "and killed a teller named Michelle."

Zygolt's chest heaved.

"That's goddamn awful!" she said. "Michelle? We knew her. Remember, guys?"

"Woman who helped us trace the lost check?" Marcus said. "She was way super cool. For a teller."

"She always wanted to see us perform," Clytemnestra said. "Now she never will. What a sucking waste."

Zygolt thumb-wiped her eyes and shook her head.

"Do you want to do something about it?" I asked. "And help your own careers? Showbizzers, let's break a leg and crush crime.'

Zygolt went back into her Showbizzer boss style.

"How does this help our careers as artists?" she asked.

"Curiosity," I said. "In the history of everything, this has not happened before. How old do you think policing is?"

"Like whoring," Clytemnestra said. "Been around forever."

"Since 1829," I said. "That's less than 200 years. How many artists ever worked as cops?"

They looked at each other and shrugged.

"Very few," I said. "George Orwell, Eddie Egan, Dennis Farina, Dorothy Uhnak."

"I never heard of any of them," Marcus said. "Farina, maybe."

"Not a one," Clytemnestra said. "Except maybe that Farina also."

"Not even George Orwell?" Zygolt said. "Marcus, you've got to stop reading comedies and start reading books."

"I'll google them," Koy said.

"That's what will help you," I said. "I'm not one of you Showbizzers. But I heard that in showbiz, you've got to have a gimmick. Something that makes you stand out from the others. Am I right?"

"Doesn't mean to get your butt shot off," Zygolt said. "And that's where this mother-kissing sales talk is going, I'm afraid."

"I'm starting to feel like I'm selling vacuum cleaners," I said.

"Really?"

"Door to door," I said.

Everyone except Snowball, Koy and I were passing around the joint and smoking it. It looked as big as a hot dog roll smoldering red at the tip.

"Door-to-door to grumpy housewives," I said.

"Well, at least, you can do something with a damn vacuum cleaner," Marcus said. "With a feeling of being a good citizen, Boy Scout type, unpaid crime fighter, I'm not sure that you can take that to the bank."

"Don't mention the word 'bank', please," Zygolt said. She shivered.

"What did I say?" Marcus asked. "I say something wrong?"

"I'm trying to reach across the generations here," I said.

"Why?" Zygolt said. "I'm older than you. I'm 56."

"Max looks older," Marcus smirked.

"If you do this work and crack any kind of case," I said, "the media will eat it for dinner. They will want to see the artists who sacrificed for society. And you are not government types. You can brag. You can give interviews. Government cops need to get permission to be interviewed."

"If we're not dead," Koy said, reading her computer. "You still didn't pay me for the gas, Max."

"You can claim credit," I said. "You can self-promote. The public, everyone, will want to look into your eyes. You won't be just another skinny unknown artist. And Snowball can be as popular as Lassie."

When he heard his name, Snowball reared up on his legs and barked.

"There's one endorsement," I said. "George Orwell went into the Burmese Police and went on to write about it in *Burmese Days*. Then he wrote *1984* and *Animal Farm*, among other books. Eddie Egan was the street narco detective in my NYPD. He broke the French Connection case, became a police hero, then an actor and worked in movies and TV until the day he died. Dennis Farina was a Chicago cop for 18 years, became an actor and worked for 35 happy years. Dorothy Uhnak was a 21-year old Jewish female transit cop in 1953. All cops then were supposed to be big bruising Irishers from the Budweiser tribe. She turned her experiences into best-selling books and TV movies and never had to work as a cop again."

"What about dancers?" Zygolt said.

"Or dog trainers?" Koy asked.

Marijuana's thick smell filled the house now. I coughed and gagged. My bruises whined.

"Whatever your deal is, the public will hear about you and want to see you," I said. "For cheap thrills. Guaranteed."

"We can be just as cheap as they are," Zygolt said. "Okay. We'll try your whacko idea. For a week."

"A week?" I said. "What can we do in a week?"

"You'll just have to show us, won't you?" Zygolt said. "One week."

CHAPTER 12

My Very Own Police Academy

The next morning, I scribbled notes on Rules of Evidence in my room.

They looked as dull as they had in the NYPD Academy on East 20th Street. Today, that seemed like a century ago.

Dressing, I gathered the notebooks and swung my way to their house. My knee felt better now. It was healing. Everything was going to work out.

Standing to the side of the door, like the cops instructors had trained me to do, I knocked.

Nothing happened.

Morning wind picked up from the desert. It brought that same clean brushy smell of grass. Later on, the sun would heat up that grass.

My knuckles hit the wood again.

Nobody answered.

My bold plan of action was fumbling off to a wonky start.

The door opened. Marcus put his head outside.

"Is the sorry place on fire?" he grunted.

"Not yet. You guys ready for some book learning?"

"Later," he said. "Go bite yourself.'

Then he closed the door.

"Dissipation of youthful energies," I said to the door. "You're making me feel like a wellness counselor at an orgy."

When confronted by a problem like this, I followed an established plan. I returned back to bed and took a nap.

❧

Some delicious time later, I woke and gathered up my pocket notebooks. Screwing my courage to the sticking point, I hobbled back to the house.

Luckily, the door was hanging open this time. So were the Showbizzers. They were on their straw tatami mats, eating big breakfasts after their big night.

"Oh, Max," Koy groaned.

It was not a happy greeting.

"I been there, where you are now," I said. "Hangover City. I used to think that I was the mayor."

"Wisecracks might kill us today," Zygolt said. "How about tomorrow for you?"

"That vodka," Koy said. "Helps me to understand Dostoevsky better in translation."

"Then it was a literary pursuit," I said. "Who here has ever bought something that you did not need?"

"We may have bought you, for a week," Marcus said. "But I ain't sure that we need you."

It was time for our hero to keep forging ahead.

"You bought that stuff sometimes," I said, "because a salesman got you. That salesman sized you up when you approached his wares. He started an interview, to see what you THINK that you needed. But did he wind up by selling you something else?"

"You're selling us your philosophy now," Marcus said. "And you are for sure something else."

"Hey," Koy said. "We don't want to do this nonsense. Classroom learning. Quizzes. This is why we left straight society and stuff like that."

"And why we left stuff like health plans and dental insurance," Clytemnestra said. "Why my teeth hurt so often."

"Listen up, sports fans," Zygolt said. "I said that we would humor Max's crazy idea for a week. And we will do it. I'm the ramrod here."

The Showbizzers took that in. Koy's face muscles worked at hiding something. I fought not to get distracted by her eyes again.

"A good interview," I said, "is when you move a person from the chair marked 'Unwilling' to the chair marked 'Willing'. We interview every day, without thinking about it. It may be just to ask directions. I've been doing a lot of that recently. Maybe this morning, you want me to be getting directions to leave you alone. You'd like that, right?"

Nobody reacted.

I plowed on with the lesson, I could feel them slipping away. So a command decision was in order.

"That's enough about interviewing," I said. "Now, who wants to be murdered?"

They looked at each other.

"Is that part of your training program?" Zygolt asked.

"Just why did the police drop you, again?" Clytemnestra asked.

"We've finished those big hangover breakfasts, class?" I said.

"We don't call them 'hangovers' any more, Max," Clytemnestra said. "That is my parents' generation."

"What do you call them, then?" I asked.

Nobody answered.

"The French have a phrase for it," I said. "*Guelle de bois. It means 'wooden throat'.*"

"O those Frenchies," Koy said. "They ought to know. They invented wine."

"Actually, you Chinese did," I said. "We're going to learn a bit how not to get killed. Can we arise, please?"

Nobody moved.

Something went out of me. I sagged on my crutches.

"This is mutiny," I said, trying to paste a smile on my puss.

Tension grew.

"The first rule is what we should not do," I said. "We should not use our fists. Ever. We should try any grappling. We should forget wrestling. Or the movies."

"Then, goddammit all to hell, what should we do?" Clytemnestra asked.

"We should do damage and then run," I said. "We will not be cops who have to arrest somebody. We hit only when we have to, to save our lives. Then we run. And if the villain in our play tries to stop you, you keep running.

"And we don't call this class 'Self Defense' or 'Defensive Tactics' or anything like that. Because words are so very powerful. As Showbizzers, you know that. You use words to inspire yourselves, overcome fears and sell your art to the audience.

"Self Defense implies that we hang back, cover up and try a kick or two. That won't work. A street fighter knows to blitz you, come in fast and overwhelm you in seconds. He will hit you six times before you can process that you are being attacked. As soon as he does that, he beats you. You cannot recover after six hits."

"So what do we call this class?" Koy asked.

"I call it 'How-to -Hurt'," I said. "Not 'Self-Defense?'"

"Why do we keep running?" Zygolt asked. "I mean, if we know how to fight and everything?"

"We keep running because it is very hard for your attacker to run after you and keep hitting you. It just doesn't work. You should keep running. The brain overloads. Your attacker will give up."

"But, if we have to hit," I said, "we hit with this."

I put out my left hand, bent the wrist as far back as possible and curled the thumb and fingers out of the way.

"We hit with the palm. Breaking your palm is nearly impossible. Hit any surface that you want, with your palm."

I took the Basta phone book from the front desk and held it in front of my chest, leaning on my right crutch.

"Marcus, hit the book with your fist," I said. "If you please."

"I'm not really into this," he said.

"Do your best," I said. "It's in a good cause."

He stepped up, balled his fist and hit the phone book that was flush against my chest. It hit strongly. I spun a bit on the crutch.

My students sat up now. This interested them.

"Now, try the palm of your hand," I said. "Fingers curled out of the way."

He hit with the palm heel strike. This jolt felt much bigger to me.

As I had programmed, I went backwards against the sofa and onto it. The crutch fell, too.

"See?" I gasped. "The palm heel works better. From your palm to your elbow is a straight line, with no energy lost.

When you throw a fist punch, you lose much energy because of your wrist joint. And you can't hit with your knuckles as hard as with your palm. Because your knuckles will crack if you hit something hard enough. Practice on this for a while."

Their faces lit up. They practiced with the phone book.

The air still held the marijuana smell. I wondered what the sheriff would say about that.

"And now our friend the elbow," I said. "You've all got two. Use it going up to the jaw or sideways to the neck. Or downwards to the gut. Or, when you have him exposed there, smash the spine. Use it when you are close and you can't miss with it."

The knee, forearm and side of the hand followed.

"Practice this stuff when you are alone every night," I said. "Try for just five minutes. Then increase it by five minutes each time. Your hand speed will increase and you'll be able to hit with focus, even from shadow-boxing the night air."

Getting tired, we sat down again for my words on Rules of Evidence.

"Two mopes razor-cut a model in Manhattan," I said. "Five blocks away, we cops grab them based on the description of 911 callers and handcuff them. They bring the bleeding hysterical victim to the scene. She is wailing inside the ambulance now. But she identifies the men who sliced her."

"Max," Koy said.

"Sorry. When it got to trial, the learned counsel defense lawyer had her ID ruled invalid and tossed out of court. The square-John citizens in the jury never got to hear that she had identified these lovely guys. Who can tell me why?"

"The cops did not read them their Miranda rights?" Clytemnestra said. "I saw that on TV."

"Not quite. There was no need to read them. We stopped them because of eyewitnesses calling 911. The sidewalk identification was thrown out because the suspects were handcuffed at the time. The defense lawyer said, and the judge agreed, that having the suspects already handcuffed would suggest to the average victim that they were already judged to be guilty of something."

"That's outrageous," Marcus said.

"No, it's not," I said. "It's just the reason that we're having this class."

"Just drop them off the top of a building," Koy said.

They looked at me sorrowfully.

"Clytemnestra mentioned Miranda Rights," I said. "The good news is that we are civilians and do not have to give suspects Miranda Rights. If they talk, we can listen, remember it and repeat it in court. We only have to obey the law. We do not have to worry about procedure, department politics, budgets, what our bosses will say or any of that other crud."

"Why don't we have to worry about procedure or any of that mess?" Koy asked.

"Because all those rules about procedure are for the government. We are not government."

"Not hardly," Marcus said.

"Let me not sound too dry," I said. "The law has what it calls 'a silver platter doctrine'. That means that you, a private citizen, can get evidence any which way you can, bring it before the court, and the judge can act on it."

"So what?" Zygolt said.

"So, you think someone's dealing crack out of his house. You break into his crib, take the crack and you and the cops put it before a judge for a search warrant. The court does not have to know how you got it. They can just issue the warrant."

"Oh, I like this!" Clytemnestra said. "We can break into places and not get caught. I always wanted to be a lady cat burglar."

"Max, that seems crazy," Marcus said.

"Check with any criminal lawyer. They'll back me up. All the rules are for cops. Not us."

"I've heard," Zygolt said, "of kids breaking into their parents' bedroom and finding drugs, bringing the drugs to court and getting a search warrant and the cops busting their parents. It's like that?"

"Just like that," I said. "Remember, I'm just giving you the basics in this course. And the law may change. So the courses will continue."

"Why?" Koy said. "Some of it is way boring."

"Koy," Zygolt said.

"Because the more I train you," I said, "the less chance that you'll be arrested or sued. A lawsuit judgment can take all your assets and payments for your art for the next seven years."

"Because they will call us vigilantes?" Clytemnestra said.

"You already called me one," I said. "Because the government does not want citizens doing what we are about to try. They will discourage us any way that they can. In America, anyone can sue anyone else. Someone that you investigate can sue you and tie you up in court for years. So we'll try staying hidden."

"It's frightening, what we're trying to do," Marcus said.

"I agree," I said. "But it is controlled danger. That's why I'm teaching you and boring you today."

Zygolt made a face, rolled her eyes and put on her dazzling smile again. For an instant, she looked like a teenager again.

"We'll tackle Going Undercover later on," I said. "Marcus and Clytemnestra, you'll be training us all on that. As actors, you know about researching a role and learning your character's motivation."

"This is going to be a long week," Koy pouted. "Full of craparoo man myths."

"I can see that you're going to be the class problem child," I said.

She stuck out a pink tongue at me.

"There are longer weeks," I said. "In jails. In hospital ward rooms because you did not hurt the other guy fast enough. Remember that I'm just teaching you the basics. If anyone here thinks that they know more than a rookie deputy on his beat, you won't last long on the street. It is more efficient to teach smart people to become investigators than it is to try teaching investigators to become smart people."

CHAPTER 13

Night Stuff

"Well, that was a lousy damn day!" Clytemnestra said.

The desert sun was setting over the scrub.

"You, the schoolmaster!" Clytemnestra glowed. Her cheeks bunched over her pointed chin. Her blue eyes reflected her blue jeans and denim work shirt. Her red hair hung down after her shower, and she smelled of fresh soap and the leather from her new brown belt.

We were sitting on the stoop of their home, facing my building.

Chick, the concierge, passed in front of us. He dragged a shovel with a red steel handle behind him.

"The other Showbizzers are quiet now," I said. "Maybe tired out."

"Reading or sleeping is my guess," she said. "You remember hangover days, don't you?"

"Painfully. When did you know that you wanted to be an actress, Clytemnestra?"

"Every actress wants a national talk-show host to ask her that very same question."

"You'll have to settle for crutchy, stout me," I said. "In Basta."

"In grammar school, I played Eliza Doolittle in *My Fair Lady*. That's when it first hit me. And people would pay me for this, if I got good enough."

"As far back as that?"

"Yeah. Everything else followed. The teachers who put together plays knew that they had a sucker for studying lines. So they piled the stuff on me."

"You said that you parents were hippies?"

"Some of the fake-Woodstock hippie zeal had died out by the time that I came around," she said. "My Dad worked part-time helping a baker, and my Mom was slaving at the phone company. Nothing that I wanted for me. Four other kids with me, one with autism, so this was no easy life to pay the bills. I learned real early that money makes the world go around. Money comes right before drugs and sex. Sex will sell when cotton won't."

She leaned against the doorpost, holding a Budweiser can in her hand.

"I acted all through high school and junior college," she said. "Waited tables while doing it. I told myself that every new customer was just like a new play."

"Very like," I said.

"As soon as I can, I'll go cruise those crummy bars for talk on the murder. I know that I was rushing out the door to do it."

"I noticed."

"One of my therapists said that I cannot keep to a plan of action. That I suffer from Attention Deficit Disorder. Among other things."

"Please don't do it until you're ready."

"I know that you've got the hots for Koy," she said.

"I guess that the serenading gave away the element of surprise," I said.

"You're wasting your time."

"I have plenty of it to waste."

"She is beautiful, no question about that, my friend. But she has a boyfriend. Chinese. And a chemical engineer. Her future is secured and locked down."

"And I bet that he has a better wardrobe than I have at the moment."

"Max, you don't have a wardrobe."

"Clothes-shopping on crutches without a car can be challenging."

"I'll take you shopping. We agreed amongst us that when we rented this house that we would not date any of the locals. Sooner or later, there would be a scene and a breakup and we'd have people whispering about us in town. Sex and drugs or some damn nonsense. And we aren't interested in the Basta-type of man anyway. Beer, Jeeps and sweaty sex. Did you know that only eleven percent of Basta folks have four-year college degrees? What do they do, for Chrissake?"

"Beer and sweaty sex."

"Damn betcha. Must be."

"And who makes your heart beat just a little bit faster these days?"

"Me. Just me. At Christmas time, I broke up with my boy-friend and got through an abortion without any help from him, thank you very much. So I'm benching myself for this goddamn season. There's been enough hacked-off mad regrets for me."

"There's always next season."

Footsteps sounded above us. Marcus came downstairs barefoot and shirtless. His solid arm muscles bunched and tensed as he leaned towards us, gripping the doorframe.

"Marcus," I said, just to be polite. "What are you up to?"

"Cocaine. Want some? Scored enough for another hit."

"Coke," I said. "Is that to forget about today's class? Or to get ready for tomorrow's?"

"Well, your sorry old class on evidence did run a little dry. Damn, Bubba."

"You're the creative ones," I said. "The bright light of civilization in the dark wood of the world. You are the force that brought mankind out of the caves and towards knowledge. If you just swallow my boring lectures and do nothing to make them different, do you know what will happen?"

"I got no damn clue. What?"

"We'll wind up in the caves again. And it'll be your fault."

"Max, sometimes you talk like a man with a paper asshole."

"That sounds cowboy to my Manhattan ears. Where is home, Marcus?"

"El Paso, Texas. 600,000 Texicans with only one legitimate theater. I had to bust out. Someday, they'll hear of me."

"Pardon the cleesh," I said.

"What?"

"O generation of youths," I said. "You can't know it but you just gave out every cliché for young unknown actors."

"Well, it's true."

"They always are."

"Take a hit, Max. It'll bring our sorry little group closer together."

"Marcus, I'm sending out bundles of lawyer letters, trying to gripe my way back into the New York cops. They will test me for drugs and I need that pension."

"I thought that you already had it."

"Marcus, if I already had it, would I be trying to get back into the Department?"

"Yes, you would," Zygolt spoke up.

She came onto the stoop from the living room.

"Seems to me to be the kind of messianic, dedicated personality who can become goddamn obsessive. With whatever he fixates upon."

"Lay on the couch, patient, and tell me all about your dreams," I said.

"And, at this moment, you're all fixated on this dumb concept of yours, to turns us into ticket-writing, doughnut-munching cops."

"Not hardly, Zygolt. The average police department in this country is an inside joke. A collection of bullies, good cops, high school jocks, toxic supervisors and kids trying to decide which one they will be."

"So why should we join them?" Marcus asked.

"You don't," I said. "You lead them. With your superior creativity and command of language, you feed them ideas."

"They'll laugh at an actor trying to play cop," Marcus said.

"But not at your ideas. Not if they work. If they work, the cops will steal them and call them their own."

"Going to be a long week," Clytemnestra said. "Marcus, you hunk you, you really have enough for one more hit of that coke?"

"For you, housemate, any time."

"This is some team of crime fighters that I've fallen into," I said.

"The goodies are upstairs," Marcus said.

"Let's go then," Clytemnestra said.

They scampered up the stairs, holding hands.

"Well!" I said, hamming it up.

"Shocked, Max?" Zygolt asked.

"These kids today, I tell you."

"Yeah. They make me feel old sometimes, too. That was a bland damn dinner. We already ate up all those Middle Eastern treats that you used to bribe us and hear your ideas. Tricky, Max."

"I have no idea what you're talking about. Where did you all meet?" I asked.

"I was teaching Modern Dance at the University of California at Riverside near here. My ex-husband tried to open a dance studio here in Basta. Rented this house from Chick. Basta has so much need for the skateboarding druggy kids here just to get exposed to art. Everything here goes too fast – driving, slamming beers, football and marrying too young. I'm a believer in the healing power of art."

"You mentioned your husband."

"Just not in my life anymore."

"I'm sorry," I said.

"Don't be. I knew that he was bisexual when I married him. But he's a wonderful, warm, laughing fun kind of person. You and him could real happily close down a bar together."

"Get him over here, then. There's a few Basta bars that need exploring."

"When he left, Basta seemed to have potential. Something contrary in me didn't want to leave just because my husband fell in lust with some truck driver. So I advertised for housemates in the arts. Building an arts community in this Mojave Desert really floats my boat. Marcus showed up first. I told him right up front, no romance. The last thing that I goddamned needed was some more ambiguous sex. Even with our age difference, I needed to make that clear before I could let him pay rent."

"Does he have a heartthrob nearby?"

"An ex visits him from Pasadena sometimes. She wants marriage; he wants Hollywood. They'll explode pretty soon. Then Koy and her boyfriend were driving through with Snowball in the back seat."

Hearing about that boyfriend again pulled me back to high school jealousy.

"Are they going to explode pretty soon, too?" I asked.

She smiled her full-wattage smile again.

"Why do you ask?" she said.

With all the dignity of a beer belly on crutches, I arose and paced about the room.

"Koy feeds Snowball every night, walks him, takes a blasting hot shower and is asleep in her pajamas by nine," Zygolt said. "She's a traditional girl. You probably won't see her again tonight."

"Yup," I said. At times, I can be very suave.

It was full dark now. The crescent moon would be coming up soon.

"You Showbizzers have guessed my feelings about Koy," I said. "I have to be more subtle. Jealousy could wreck our experiment. So could favoritism. Koy seems to want me to go alone to Bora-Bora Island in the South Pacific and be subtle there. Doesn't seem that she would miss me."

"It's groovy to hear a man speak so openly," she said. "Most men don't. It turns me on."

"And friend Clytemnestra?" I asked.

"Going through de-tox, and her counselor warned her to get out of Las Vegas before she fell back into old habits again. A quiet desert town seemed like a good place to re-build her psyche. But you already saw the dark side of Basta. She played in *Cats* and *Hedda Gabler* in Claremont. But they were showcases without any pay. She may be forced to go to L.A. unless something happens here."

The name of Crosswaite floated across my mind just then.

But Zygolt shook her head and got my attention.

"You should change your teaching style," Zygolt said.

"That bad, huh?"

"I had a minor in sociology," she said. "Thought that was dull and dry and pedantic. Then you came along, with your piss-faced Rules of Evidence lesson."

Once again, I felt as if I were ten-years old and back in that sailor suit.

"I'll change my style tomorrow morning," I said.

"How?"

"I don't know."

"You are one nutty bunny," she said. "Come upstairs with me. I'll show you my room."

Her smile came back.

She cocked her head at me.

"Just because I'm alone now," she said, "it doesn't mean that I want to be."

To gain myself time, I started to fake a cough.

"Come on, Max," she said. "What're you waiting for?"

That was a good question.

Trying for the innocent Huckleberry Finn look, I shrugged. Zygolt looked sensual right now, mature and wise and as slim as the dancer that she was. Her eyes smoked, giving her a bedroom look.

"I'm trying to form this Showbizzer team," I said. "Treating everyone the same."

"Do you think that you're doing that with Koy?" she said. "Or maybe you think that I'm too flipping old to be your lover. Imagine how that makes me feel."

She passed by me and went upstairs. Her door slammed. In her room, her steps paced back and forth.

I slunk back to my rented room, locked the door and fell onto the bed.

CHAPTER 14

Elegance

"Celebration, my Showbizzers!" I said on Saturday morning. "I'm proud of you. You all passed your courses."

"Whoopee," Marcus said. "Now we are all Junior G-men."

"And, kids," I said. "Guess where Daddy Max is taking you today? Someplace highly cultural."

"Abbey Theater?" Clytemnestra asked.

"Pasadena Playhouse?" Marcus asked. "It's a shorter commute."

"Westminster Kennel Club?" Koy asked.

"The parking lot outside the Desert Market," I said. "Highly cultural."

"Aw, cowflop," Clytemnestra said. "Can you see me doing my fly imitation there?"

She pinched her face into a grimace, hunched her shoulders and rubbed one forearm against the other. Her top teeth bit on her lower lip. She transformed herself. She looked exactly like a fly on someone's leg. It made me feel itchy.

"You're good," I said. "Great improv actress."

"So long as we get the damn money," she said.

"All the money," Koy said.

"Marcus, please throw those muscles into play," I said. "Hoist my duffle bag into the Roadmaster. I warn you, it's heavy."

"Don't rupture yourself, cowboy," Clytemnestra the fly whooped. "It's Saturday morning heading into a heavy weekend."

"Zygolt," I said. "Like the country folks say, today I'm the man with the plan."

Zygolt looked at me, chilled me with those eyes and looked away.

My head dipped down. It was an old boxer's reflex, whenever anything hit you. You tucked your head lower so that the next punch might hit your forehead and not your eye.

Zygolt was still steamed that I had stayed out of her bedroom last night. Maybe she did not understand the loneliness of command.

"Today is a day for surprises!" I said, forcing a happy note in my voice. "We're heading to our graduation party."

"At the Desert Market?"

"First, put these on," I said. I dug into a shopping bag. Skyblue T-shirts came out onto my hand. I pitched one underhanded to Clytemnestra.

She squealed and caught.

"Oh!" She read the lipstick-colored letters stamped on her shirt. "'Basta Showbizzers!' How cool!"

"It's not my color," Zygolt said.

"Of course it is!" Koy said. "It matches your eyes."

Clytemnestra stripped off her man's work shirt. She wore a narrow black bra holding in her breasts over a flat stomach and narrow hips. Marcus grinned, lips skinning back and dark eyes glowing. Zygolt frowned. Clytemnestra put on the new Basta Showbizzers shirt. The medium size fit her slim body.

"We tried this publicity routine before," Zygolt said. "It died of a Monday."

"Today's Saturday," I said. "Full of promise. Last one in the car is an untalented wage-slave!"

❧

Snowball stuck his wooly white head out the Roadmaster window and drooled pinkly all the wet way to the Desert Market.

Cool breezes from the night before still blew. Tumbleweeds bounced and rolled and flipped by the road. The desert smelled clean. A turkey buzzard drifted on thermals, high overhead.

We parked near the front entrance and put the tailgate down. The others changed into the Showbizzers T-shirts.

"Those shirts are binding us into becoming a team," Marcus said.

"We were a team before these crummy shirts," Zygolt said. "I feel like taking mine off."

I ignored that. Maybe life would be easier if I started serenading Zygolt instead of Koy.

Shoppers in bluejeans, Stetson hats and loose shirts were jumping ahead of the Saturday crowds. It was just past nine a.m.

Marcus shucked out his guitar from the car. He started playing "The William Tell Overture." The notes climbed over the parking lot.

Koy started Snowball leaping up and then rolling over. Snowball played dead and then jumped up. Shoppers cheered.

Snowball ate up the applause, stopped in an instant and then rolled over three times. Koy's face lit up. She shouted commands.

My hands put a CD into the dashboard player. Cowboy guitar music flowed out.

"What is that?" Marcus asked. "I'm getting upstaged. That means fighting, where I come from."

"That's Johnny Western singing the song 'Bonanza', I said. "After that, he does 'The Ballad Of Paladin'."

"Max, how did you find these songs?"

"They found me. On TV. When I was about six years old, in New York City."

I unrolled a wide tagboard sign that read "Free Dog-Washing and Tick Check By Koy, Certified Animal Trainer."

"Free?" Koy asked.

"That'll suck them in first," I said. "No real American can resist anything marked 'Free' for six consecutive minutes. Watch me prove it."

Leaning on the tailgate, I took a small cast-iron grill out of the duffle bag. Dry kindling went into the grill.

I set it on the ground near the Roadmaster.

"And what are you going to do with that?" Koy asked.

"Something very New York," I said.

"Showbizzers, break a leg and crush crime."

"Max," Koy said, using my name. She rarely called me by name. It stretched my smile. "I don't know if you've noticed this."

"Noticed what, my dear?" I asked.

"I am not your dear. And Basta has a lot of rednecks dragging mangy, filthy dogs around on clotheslines."

"I've noticed. In Manhattan, those same of dogs ran in wild packs in the 'hood. Locals there call them 'ghetto elk'."

"And you want me washing these filthy mutts for free?"

"For love," I said. "Because you love so much."

"I do?"

ↄ

Twenty minutes later, when I came out of the Desert Market with another shopping bag, there were three owners with their dogs waiting for the free wash-and-tick check. All of them, dogs and owners, looked like they needed a hot bath and a shower of flea powder.

Clytemnestra was uncoiling a garden hose from the car and running it to a spigot on the Desert Market wall.

"Whatcha got in the bag, Max?" she asked.

"Remember, my Showbizzers," I said, faking a snooty voice. "We are artists, true artists."

"Only if con men are artists," Koy said.

"And, everything that we true artists do," I rolled on, "we do with elegance. Elegance, above all."

"So whatcha got in the bag?"

"Kosher hot dogs and Dijon mustard," I said. "We'll get the grill going hot in a couple of minutes."

"What if our local audience-of-the-future don't like hot dogs?" Zygolt said. "What are you going to feed them then?"

"Pig's feet. In brine. Here's the jumbo jar. They're making the jars out of plastic now so they won't break."

"Oh, that would never do," Zygolt said.

The smell of hot dogs grilling over wood smoke drew the men in the shopping couples.

"He's a beautiful dog," Koy said to the owners. "We can send you some more of this soap for free. Just put your name and email here on the clipboard. Or your phone, if you wish."

"I don't know about that," a big rancher-type said. He wore a cracked straw Stetson and a mud-colored leather belt trimmed in white rope.

"Oh, sure!" Clytemnestra beamed at him, leaning in closer. "What are you worried about? There's nothing to be afraid of with us."

The man, inhaling her, seemed to agree. He signed his name, email and spent some time talking crops with her.

Hot dogs kept rolling off the grill and into local bellies.

Deputy Enrique Mendoza swung by in his patrol car. He ogled Koy soaping down a liver-colored mutt, shook his head and drove away.

"We've got some extra T-shirts to give away!" I shouted over Johnny Western's voice singing "The Alamo."

"We do?" Clytemnestra asked.

"Sure," I said. "What size are you, sir?"

"I ain't buying no silly shirt," he said.

"You're right, sir," I said. "You're not. It's free. Please take this 2XXL for yourself."

"Always worry about things I get for free," he said. "How can you give stuff like this away?"

I looked around for eavesdroppers.

"Government grant," I said.

He nodded his bulldog head and left.

The words "government grant" could explain everything.

A man with a handlebar moustache and a brightly shaved head came out of the Desert Market. He wore a light gray smock, the words "Assistant Manager" stenciled over his breast.

"I'm Randy Solba, the Assistant Manager," he said. "Are you gypsies?"

"Please look at the blonde lady and ask that," I said. "Do you see a lot of blonde gypsies?"

"Does anybody else see blonde gypsies?" Clytemnestra asked. "Or is it just you? Have you thought about getting some professional help?"

"Excuse me?" Randy-the-Assistant-Manager said.

"If you need a shrink," Clytemnestra said, "I can recommend some bad ones."

Randy Solba shook his head again.

"Who are you people?" he asked again.

"Customers," I said. "These here are your own hot dogs from the frozen meat section. Do you want mustard on yours?"

"You can't set up a business in my parking lot."

"We're not. We're just washing dogs."

"And using my water from that outlet. Without permission."

"Well, Randy, you can give us permission now, can't you?"

"But I won't. You're stealing water. In the desert. Shut that off!"

Just like in Patrol, I dropped my voice down way low.

"Now, Randy, we'll be gone in a half hour," I said. "Thirty little minutes. See those doggies lined up for a washing? Each owner is a the Desert Market customer. Do you want me to tell them that the Desert Market won't let them get their dog washed for free? How will that sound? I can do it, if that's what you want."

He glared.

"Or we can do nothing," I said, "and just be gone in thirty minutes. Out of your life. You don't want customers saying that you're anti-canine, do you, Randy?"

"I'm going to –"

"Twenty-nine minutes now, Randy. It'll be okay, pal. Trust me. And thanks."

More locals walked away with clean dogs, holding new T-shirts. Johnny Western batted out the song "Johnny Yuma, The Rebel," over the CD player.

Soapsuds covered Koy's bare strong arms. She worked the scrub brush over a scrawny mutt that looked part German shepherd and part Labrador retriever. Koy's wide white smile flashed under her tanned skin and black hair.

Taking in a deep breath and girding my loins, I spoke to Zygolt.

"Oh, no!" she said. "No way! Dream on!"

"Come on. Try."

"It's too early. This is a conservative redneck town. The sun has to go down and beer has to flow before anyone can have a good time."

"Come on, Zygolt. You're the one who wants Basta kids to know about art."

"Not this way."

"Is the other way working?" I asked.

I tried to give her my best Showbizzer smile and then walked back to the car and changed Johnny Western to another CD, "Ghost Riders in the Sky."

"What's that honky-tonk stuff?" Clytemnestra asked. "Shitkicker stuff."

"It's not honky-tonk," I said. "It's Western Swing. Listen to that delicate fiddle."

"Not sure that I like it."

"You don't have to. The audience does."

I grilled and gave away more hot dogs.

When I looked up again, Zygolt had about nine locals in rows around her.

"Now, we'll start our first line-dance lesson," Zygolt said. "Get your weight on your left foot and spin around. We'll dance to the tune of 'Pink Cadillac' on the CD player."

The locals spun and danced, following Zygolt. Some whooped. They were not waiting for sunset to enjoy themselves.

"This is the only way to shop!" one shouted. She sported one of our T-shirts stretched over her body. Huge thighs bunched and flexed in her watermelon-colored shorts.

"I'm torn-down exhausted," Koy said, coming up. But she beamed her wide smile.

Working dogs joyed her.

"Are we going to have to do this every Saturday?" she said.

CHAPTER 15

Romance Undercover

Night covered our driveway.

"Marcus," I said. "How often do you pump iron?"

"Try for twice a week, Max. Goddamn it to hell. You know what? You just reminded me that I missed my last workout. Now, I'm finer than frog hair and rarin' to go."

"All lifters always remember that they missed their last workout," I said. "It's just a question of me reminding you when. Juggling my crutches here, can I try lifting with you?"

"Yup. Sometimes Koy and Cly join me. But today it's just us fellas? How often do you lift?"

"Anything's better than push-ups," I said. "Push-ups and me have agreed a long time ago to hate each other. Can't stand putting my mug on the ground."

"I'll bring my set now. You just take it easy here."

He brought out two barbells, forty pounds each, and a long bar with two plates reading "60 LBS."

"D'you really think that I can toss off curls with forty-pounders?" I asked. "Is that coke still in your system or something?"

"Overload principle, bubba. Lift more than you can."

"There is a paradox in there somewhere," I said.

We sat on crates in the shadow of the Showbizzer house. Maybe the crates were authentic Route 66 garbage and worth a lot to collectors. I would have to ask Chick.

Moving only my arms, I warmed up what was left of my body, still sitting on the valuable crate.

"Jab, jab, hook, cross," I panted. "Come on, old body. Don't get lazier than you are."

"You were a boxer?"

"Never," I said. "If I tried it, I would be graveyard dead now. It is just something that pulls me more than running on a treadmill."

"That's like me with football. El Paso is crazy about football."

"Two more minutes to warm up.

Never work a cold body."

My fists felt like they belonged to someone else. My wrist and forearm bones seemed to rattle against the skin.

"Hiya, Foxy Maxy," Zygolt said, coming out of the doorway. "Today's Monday. Been playing cop for a week and got damn-all nothing to show for it."

My fists stopped.

"We agreed on a week," Zygolt went on. "You got your week."

"Oh, brother," Marcus said.

My teeth sucked in. It was more of the charming habits stuck to me from Patrol.

Not trusting my voice, I just pulled myself up and onto my crutches again.

Zygolt was still in her bathrobe, a wine-colored claret shade of light cotton. Maybe she could not wait to end our experiment together today.

Trying to slow my speech rhythm down from fast-talking New Yorker, I made myself stretch my arms and spine on the crutches.

"Zygolt, can we go into a huddle for a sec?" I asked.

"Why? We can talk in front of Marcus. Keeping secrets, never my style."

"It's me," I said. "I might be too shy to speak in front of a pro actor like Marcus. He might criticize my character's motivation or my delivery."

Zygolt mouthed an obscene gerund.

I made way around the corner of the house, with her trailing me.

"Zygolt, I keep forgetting. Where is home for you?"

"Don't matter. What did you want to talk about that's so private?"

"How many plays have you put on in Basta so far?"

"Max, the four of us, we've only been here three months. We've done two showcases for kids and have five acting students. Sweating horsehair to get more."

"Word-of-mouth helps, Zygolt. Clytemnestra got thirty-one names and emails from Bastas with dirty dogs on Saturday. We gave out twenty-three T-shirts that are being stretched over local tummies as we speak."

"What the hell good is that for us?"

"Because we are going to doggy-wash our way to stardom," I said. "That's thirty-one emails that we didn't have before. We can hit them with emails every time that you run a dance clinic and sign up kids for lessons."

"We can't do that," Zygolt said.

"What do we have to lose?"

"Our lives. This cruddy house. Any future dance program we can put together here."

"Zygolt, why are you vexed at me?"

She did not answer. I sensed an opening.

"Ever since Friday night," I went on. "I value your friendship. I would not want to lose it, for any reason."

"Oh, yeah?"

She was still steamed.

"Zygolt, my ideas on policing back in New York cost me my career. And my pension. Can't I get your help to try those ideas in Basta and make a real change?"

She crossed her ankles and dug a toe in the ground. It was a dancer's move, something I had seen on the outdoor stage at Lincoln Center.

"One more week," she said. Then she walked back into the house, in her claret bathrobe.

Marcus was sweating and grunting by the time I got back. He cleared both barbells at once and did curls with them. It made my arms ache to watch him.

"Watch the oldster warm up again," I said. "It's Old-Timers' day at Yankee Stadium."

Sitting back down, I threw more punches. It still felt kooky, like I was way out of shape.

Then I started lifting weights alongside him, back on my crate.

It hurt. My arms protested.

"How's your money?" I asked. "Would you like a million dollars?"

"Everyone says that you're silly, Max. Belong in the home for the bewildered. I used to stick up for you. Not no more. Damn. You are silly."

"Hilarious," I said. I put the weights down and threw three more lazy jabs. "I'd like to ask you to do something. No other actor ever did this."

"That's flipping impossible. To scratch out a crummy living, actors have done everything."

"I would ask you if you got the stones to work undercover."

His dark eyes lit up.

"Where?" he asked.

"In the bank that just got robbed. Maybe this joker Cross-waite did it. You might pick up stuff that the cops never got."

"Drop dead," he said.

"Now, when you say 'drop dead', what exactly do you mean?"

"Banks bore me silly. Why you think that I turned actor? No way, Bubba."

"Banks are not boring when someone just killed a teller in this one," I said. "And there may be talk there that could help us get the killer."

"Yeah. And there might not be. So I get bored to death for months for nothing. No, Max. Dream on."

"Marcus, we'll crack this case and get media attention and interviews and awards and fan letters. And then you will wish that you were in the center of the investigation. That's where the glory is. And going undercover sounds glamorous to the public."

He watched me hoist the barbell over my head and touch it to the back of my neck. Both my arms stung.

"Big hairy long shot, man. No guarantee that I'll get anything."

"Lady customers in the bank will like you a lot. After they trust you with their cash, they'll trust you with everything else."

"Banks got jacked-up regulations about employees not dating customers. And we have a rule here in this house, against dating locals."

"Then get yourself taken prisoner and seduced."

"Not for me, man."

"It's discipline, yes," I said. "But can't discipline help you as an actor?"

"You know it can."

"Not far from here, a dyslexic hearing-impaired teenaged car thief looked at acting. His own mother had him declared 'incorrigible' in court. He was a wild one, drinking, stealing cars, always getting in fights. Cops put him in Chino Juvenile Hall for a long stretch. He knew that he needed discipline. So, when he got out, he joined the Marines and learned discipline that way. He mustered out after three years and tried acting. His Marine Corps training helped. In a few years, he was the highest paid film actor in the world."

"That's not working in a bank," Marcus said.

"It's sacrificing for something. When is your next acting job?"

"Nothing yet."

"Then try this."

"Who was that lucky actor who got so famous?"

"He wasn't that lucky," I said. "Worked hard, learned his craft and died of cancer at age fifty. Steve McQueen."

"Seen his movies."

"He wasn't the only one to translate Marine Corps discipline into acting skills. The actor Lee Marvin said that he learned how to act in the World War II Marine Corps. Said that he had to pretend to act tough and unafraid and confident in the middle of hell. And other actors spouted the same things. Harvey Keitel, Jonathan Winters, Don Addams and thousands of others. Take the interview. You chicken or something? No damn guts? No drive? What do you have to lose?"

"Maybe you right, boy," he said. "You know what they call actors who are afraid to take chances?"

"What?"

"Nothing. They die unknown."

Lifting the barbells and talking tired me out.

"Okay," he said. "I'll take the sorry old interview."

"Thanks," I said.

"Don't talk me into nothing else," he said. "Not for a damn long while."

ↄ

After I showered and napped, I ate crackers and canned tuna on my stoop, listening to the desert noises.

Clytemnestra came by, looking local in tight blue jeans, a San Diego Padres T-shirt and baseball hat. Her eyes sparkled from liquor.

"Found out that Basta bars are full of grabby funky old men," she said. "But no crime info. Here I go, out again."

That night, I went through our email addresses, looking for any Crosswaite. Nothing showed.

ↄ

The next morning, Marcus left before breakfast in the Roadmaster. He wore a dark blue dress suit, white shirt, dull tie and shined black shoes. Clearly, this was the suit that he kept for auditions. He looked like a young Congressman, dressed to take on Washington.

My whole body ached from the weightlifting yesterday. So I went back to sleep.

At breakfast, Clytemnestra, looking sleepy from her bar-hopping, gave me her handwritten notes. The barflies talked about gangs in Victorville, forty miles away, and about kids breaking into cars here. They blamed it on Mexicans. Nothing much changed in policing.

My knee hurt worse so I stayed off it and emailed my doctor in New York on Cly's computer. I begged him for a local doctor who would take my insurance.

In reply, I heard an eloquent nothing.

ↄ

A few days later, someone knocked at my window at sundown. Marcus stood there grinning in his audition suit.

"You're looking at a Temporary Interim Teller," he said. "Better known as a TIT."

"Not to bankers," I said. "They got no sense of humor about such matters."

"He got the job!" Koy said, coming up with Snowball. "A financier in our midst."

The others frolicked with Snowball.

"And, in this job," I said. "You must be eager to learn, smiling gratefully and Be-a-Friend-to-Man. Play it like a young Jimmy Stewart, awkward and thankful."

"It's just temporary, until they finish my credit and background checks," Marcus said. "After work, I went to Shooter's Bar and, Melvin, the janitor, was in there doing shots. I bought him one to celebrate my new job and we got friendly."

"Good," I said. "But the staff won't drink close by. They worry about their image. Tomorrow, jot down every worker's car description. After work, cruise all the bars in Basta. It won't take you fifteen minutes. When you see one of those cars outside a bar or restaurant, go inside ready to make friends. Be a good beer-drinking buddy. Listen to gossip."

"About the holdup?"

"About everything," I said. "Especially, the holdup."

"That's sneaky," Zygolt said. "It's spying on innocent people."

"Robbery and murder of a mother of five is pretty sneaky, too," I said. "But this is how you break cases. Undercover. Showbizzers, let's break a leg and crush crime."

"If this ever gets public, Bastas will never trust us again," she said.

They nodded.

"If this goes public, it will help all of you," I said. "Just like we are debating about the morality of this here, the public will debate the same way. That gets interest up. Everyone will want to see their hero or their villain in person."

"Are you sure?"

"Audiences love to see a villain that they can hate. If it is Long John Silver, Jesse James or Hannibal Lector, it makes no difference. Trust me. Two weeks ago, Basta barely knew that you Showbizzers existed. If we break this case, all of America will know."

CHAPTER 16

I Love to Loan

"Aren't Showbizzers supposed to have cheery witty conversations at breakfast?" I asked at breakfast the next morning. "Full of sparkling wit. Not like the rest of us."

The Showbizzers looked at me.

"Well, that's your image anyway," I said.

Clytemnestra formed a horrid sucking noise with her mouth. It filled the dining room.

"Well," I said.

We kept eating our eggs, toast and potatoes.

"I've got a fun day planned," Koy said. "Who wants to come with me to Dr. Ermela?"

"What's up?"

"More tests. There are always more dang worthless tests."

"Teaching my class of three this morning," Zygolt said. "Or else, I got to eat dog food."

"Marcus is out a-banking away at his job," I said.

"I've got my therapist," Clytemnestra said.

"And we're glad that you do," Zygolt said.

It was time to take a plunge. This way, I could find out if the Showbizzers were accepting me or not.

"Koy, I could go with you?" I said.

"Huh? What do you want? No, thanks."

Those words hung in the living room. My ribs expanded and then closed. I concentrated on just that simple exercise. If I kept doing that, the hurt might go away. Maybe.

Zygolt looked out the window at the morning traffic on Main Street.

Clytemnestra made noise getting up and putting her plate in the kitchen sink.

"This is crazy," I thought. "I'm not in high school anymore. I'm not supposed to feel hurt this way."

Snowball came over to the table. He might be my only ally.

My hand was grateful to be able to rough up the fluffy clean hair on his head. Koy had washed and groomed him. It seemed unlikely that she would do that for me.

Time did not want to pass. But I wanted it to.

My right foot tapped the floor. If the other one tapped, the pain would come right from the knee.

There were other pains swirling around inside.

"Well, I think," I said, trying to drag out the words so that they sounded casual and nothing special, "that it's time to walk off this good breakfast. Thank you very much. Can I throw some cash in a hat somewhere?"

"Get you later, Max," Zygolt grinned, a cryptic kind of smile. "Don't sweat about it, old schoolmaster."

The crutches seemed too slow getting me back to my room. But I kept moving and escaped back into the butter-colored place now called home.

☙

"A highly cultural place," I said. That was my catch phrase from Saturday's Jamboree. Measured against right now, that morning now seemed happy and golden. All of us Showbizzers had worked together for something for the common good.

My face in the tiny mirror looked back at me. Desert wind and sun were cutting new lines into the skin.

The eyebrows had grown thicker. Age was showing. So was desperation.

"Tough big-city cop," I told myself. "So, so tough."

Trying to avoid the blues, I rolled onto my bed. The knee ached. Pretty soon, the scar tissue would grow over the cuts, and I could walk again without crutches.

Going back to sleep after breakfast was decadent. So I tried to do it.

The room got hotter.

Sleep kept slipping away. But I wanted it to come.

☙

Someone tapped on my window.

Koy and Snowball stood outside the window. She wore a blouse of gray cotton with black charcoal strokes and a pair of red shorts that showed long strong legs.

"You still didn't pay me for the gas," she said.

"Let me do that right now," I said.

"If you're coming, come," she said.

She was driving the Roadmaster today. Snowball clambered into the front passenger seat. Nobody asked me. Snowball put his head against the headrest and proceeded to give it a tongue-washing.

Koy drove us onto Main Street and past the town square again.

"We're going to be way early," she said more to Snowball than to me. "But I could not relax at home, thinking about this test all week and last night. How the bloody damn hell can I have cancer? The healthiest person that you ever saw. Dinner of baked fish and raw vegetables. And I never tried booze."

"Me, neither. Except when I had to."

"It's my sweet smiling, looking-great, Chinese family that is riddled with cancer."

"From what side?"

"From Mama Koy. I would rather not talk much today."

We bounced along some more.

"If you're early, let's stop at that overlook on the other side of the railroad bridge."

Koy did not seem to hear me.

But after we crossed the long black metal bridge over different railroad tracks, she slowed and stopped in a scenic overlook spot.

Thirty feet below us, the desert plains stretched all the way to the Calico Mountains.

The Roadmaster engine shut off. It ticked and then lay quiet.

Wind picked up and blew through our car.

"I can't enjoy this," Koy said. "Romantics like you get people killed."

Snowball's head turned at her tone.

So did mine.

"What did I do?" I asked. "Where did THAT come from?"

"You know."

She pulled the car back onto the roadway and drove without speaking.

❧

Her doctor's office was inside yet another strip mall. Basta's city planner seemed to love strip malls.

"Why don't you wait in the car and keep Snowball company?" she asked. "He don't like being alone in cars."

"To tell the truth, I'd like to," I said. "Enjoy the desert scenery and all."

"Then why don't you?"

"Because I know doctors' offices and their waiting rooms too well. And sometimes it is a long and painful walk from the examination room's bad news to the reality of the blue sky outside. You need your friends right away, in that waiting room."

"And that's you? You're my friend?"

"I didn't come here to keep Snowball company."

❧

The office had a dozen Bastas watching a TV game show on the wall screen.

Koy gave her name. We sat down together.

Dr. Ermela appeared right away. That was a bad sign to me. When doctors were too prompt in seeing a patient, there was often a bad reason why.

Dr. Ermela had a cascade of black hair coming down over dark skin and creamy white teeth that she showed in a smile of greeting. Her dark eyes took me in, measured me and probably found me wanting.

"Sofia will be helping us out today," Dr. Ermela said. "Just waiting for her to finish up. Why don't we go inside the examination room and get ready, Koy?"

Koy got up and went through without looking at me or giving a declaration of love.

Another young woman in a white doctor's coat and a luminous smile came through the room. I distrusted that smile right away. I did it quickly to save time. Her face was classically Latina, and the name-tag on her jacket read "Dr. Sofia Rodos."

A silver ring flashed on her right hand. Her fingernails were painted blood red. The fingernails worried me, too. I wondered if wearing painted nails during operations was medically sound.

The waiting room had a couple of *Arizona Highways* magazines and that was all.

"Saw you at the Desert Market on Saturday," a wide, white-haired woman confided. "Washing all those sweaty dogs."

"We love doing it," I said, using the editorial "we." "We'll be doing it again real soon."

Time passed on the *Arizona Highways*.

When I was not the patient, waiting rooms often put me to sleep. Today, my head dropped back against the wildlife-painted wallpaper.

But, again, I could not sleep. After all this time inside the office, Koy worried me. They were not giving her a good health award in there.

Then she was outside, with Dr. Ermela on one side and Dr. Rodos on the other. A vein quivered in Koy's neck. I could see it pulse. Her eyes hopscotched around the room.

From alleyways and street corners, that look in her eyes was familiar to me. She was looking for a way out.

The doctors murmured blandishments and smiled their white healthy smiles of good cheer. My crutches came up into my arms.

"Koy, let's go see Snowball," I said.

"Snowball," she said.

ড়

We left the air-conditioning and went back towards our car. She opened the door and Snowball bounded up, ignored her outstretched arms and relieved himself against someone's Chrysler.

Koy's face worked.

Tears stained her eyes and broke down onto her cheeks.

"Koy, do you want to talk?" I asked. The Patrol Manual said that putting the victim's name first calms victims down and reminds them who they are.

"I don't want to bother you with this," she said, pushing the words out.

"Koy, it is not a bother. It is why I came out here with you today."

"Oh, yeah?"

"Koy, why else?"

"Dr. Ermela said that they found some cancerous tissue inside me. It's got to come out. My insurance doesn't cover it."

"Can they take it out?"

"She thinks so. But it will cost me two thousand dollars out-of-pocket."

"Two thousand dollars?" I said.

"But, if I wait, they may not be able to do the operation anyway. And the rates will go up at the end of this month. It will cost me more."

"How much more?"

"They don't know. It's up to the insurance company. And I can't get a loan. I'm maxed out on that stuff. Even selling Snowball will take too much time. And I don't want to sell him anyway."

The seat felt quite awkward by now. I squirmed in it.

"Just thinking out loud," I said. "Your family?"

"They don't have that kind of money. Not that they could give me in a week."

"Two thousand round iron men," I mused. "Two thousand bucks. Maybe Marcus could steal it from the bank."

It was not a good time to ask about Koy's boyfriend.

"Don't talk to me about banks," I said. "I always wanted to rob one myself."

"Sugar-shucks," she said. "I can't even drive now, I'm too upset."

"Two grand is a month's pension for me," I lied.

I had no pension. Cats would bark before New York gave me a pension.

The seat heaved with me in it.

I had told the Showbizzers that I had no pension. Koy must have not heard it. Or else she forgot that I said it, with her own trauma. Few people really listened to others.

"I'll loan you the money," I said. "Let's go back and give them a check before the good Dr. Ermela cranks up the price more."

"You're going to loan it to me?"

"Somehow this turned into a two thousand dollar car ride. I'm carrying some emergency checks from my backpack in case I decide to buy California."

"I don't want you to loan me the money."

"Glad that we agree. But do we have any other choice?"

"I'll pay you back."

"We can always teach Snowball to pick pockets."

"You really get pension checks?"

"Like you wouldn't believe."

That was true enough. Nobody would believe it.

"Relationship counselors might argue against this loan," I said.

"But we're not in a relationship," she said.

"We're in one now," I said. "Some kind of one, anyway."

The walk back into the office seemed too quick. Both doctors came out and watched as I took out a blank check, made it out to them and signed it. Their smiles grew.

"This is so wise of you, Koy," Dr. Ermela said.

She seemed about thirty years old, too young to have this large a practice. Maybe she was a workaholic.

"Now we can schedule this operation for next week and put this behind us."

Then we were outside again.

"I'm not happy that I had to take this loan from you," Koy said. "It bothers me."

CHAPTER 17

The Other Woman

"We seem to be at breakfast again," Zygolt said the following morning.

"Happens every day," I said.

"Clytemnestra, can you go into town and pick up a parcel at the Post Office?" Zygolt asked. "We've got some dance shoes coming in. Take the Roadmaster. I'll be food-shopping with my car. Max, when will you be able to drive?"

"Not yet," I said. "Maybe in a week."

"We'll see about adding you on our insurance as an additional driver. Koy, can you pick up my student Alice at the Transportation Center? Eleven o'clock class with her."

Koy glanced away.

"A Singer family wants me to train their dog today," Koy said. "They say that noon is the only time that works for them."

"You already told them yes?"

"Uh-huh. I had no idea that you would need the car."

Zygolt said some words often heard in houses of ill repute.

"Are they paying you, at least?" Clytemnestra asked.

"First, I have to see if their dog has talent," Koy said. "If he's the right kind of dog for me."

"Isn't rent day coming soon," I asked. "And it's a big number. Any dog, you look in his left ear and you don't see daylight coming through the right ear, that's the right kind of dog for you."

"Then there's your time and your gas," Clytemnestra said. "Gotta to stop giving away the store. These rednecks will take you to the cleaners otherwise."

Koy looked stricken. It made me wonder how sheltered she had been, growing up.

"It'll work out," I said, trying to calm Koy.

Then she looked worse. Maybe she was thinking of our loan together.

"Max, this cops-and-robbers crud is gumming up our free time here," Zygolt said. "And it's not bringing in any cash. Do you really think that we can do anything this way? No power, no guns and no respect."

"'Never doubt that a small group of dedicated people can change the world'," I quoted. "'Indeed, they are the only thing that ever has.'"

"Who said that? Hitler?"

"Margaret Mead."

"And you got Clytemnestra so hooked now that she's starring in her own show, Policewoman Undercover. And, Cly, I don't mean to play the heavy housemother. But you don't need a new reason to drink more."

"You're right," Clytemnestra said. "The old reasons were good enough."

"Clytemnestra," I said. "Can you taper down some? Pace yourself with a beer that you hate? That used to work for me."

"Max, I like that liquor rush too much. If I can't get drunk, I won't do this."

I shut up. I did not want to lose her as an undercover.

"So, why do it at all?" Zygolt asked.

"I'm cruising bars to get men talking to me. I can't do it on cream soda. And they like to buy me drinks. Brings out their inner daddy."

"That's sneaky," Koy said. "You pretending to be their friend. Just so that you can pump them for information."

"Easter's coming soon," I said. "But this Easter, there are five kids and a widower who don't have their mama or wife anymore. Killing her to get twenty-seven-K is pretty sneaky. If we have to tell lies to barflies to find this killer, I'll do it."

"It feels slimy."

"Maybe we should ask the family what they think," I said. "And, getting back to cash, I am helping you there, too."

The Showbizzers looked disgruntled.

"Because of my whacky crime-fighting idea," I said. "Marcus is working in a bank.

"For now."

"That's got to bring money into this house," I said. "What was he bringing in here before that?"

"Sex appeal," Clytemnestra said.

"Cly!"

"I like the boy," Clytemnestra said. "What's wrong with that?"

"You like all the boys."

"What's wrong with that?"

"If we keep doing as we do," I said. "Something will break. Zygolt, did you ever have a dance routine that you just could not get, no matter what you did?"

"Too flipping many of them."

"And what did you do?"

"I rehearsed them."

"Right," I said. "And kept rehearsing them. Until you felt very silly. Right?"

"How did you know?"

"I do ballroom. You did it until it felt stale. Is that how you remember it?"

"Yes. Often I'd go to sleep and dream about the routine."

"And the next day, when you tried it?"

"Sometimes, rehearsing did it. And it seemed easier to dance the steps."

"Good," I breathed out. "You've got it. That's just what we're doing, Zygolt. We're rehearsing our steps. Talking to people the right way. Active listening breaks more cases than anything else. Forget what you might see on TV, more crimes are solved this way than by forensics, polygraphs, computers and all the rest of it."

Zygolt looked past me at the kitchen.

"See about that," she said. "After the rent day. Somebody's got to run this place."

"Absolutely," I said. "Otherwise, you got an-NAR-chy."

"You mean AN-ar-chy?" Clytemnestra said.

"Koy, can you please take me to these dog-owners with you?" I asked. "I shower regularly but I still need airing out."

"Maybe you'll buy your own car when you can drive," Koy said. "Really get into the Southern California life-style."

"This is your home base, Koy?" I asked.

"No. Guangzhou, China. Like I told you before. But we moved to Los Angeles when I was three."

"Excuse me," I said. "But what is 'SoCal?'"

"Southern California," Clytemnestra said.

"All of California be nuts, yo," Zygolt said. She was swinging into rapper talk. It felt better that she was joshing with us, instead of giving orders. "A quarter of the whole state sandy worthless desert. But the ones who decided to live in the desert hate it."

"And, for more of this civics class," Clytemnestra said. "Californians don't use the land given them. Ninety-eight percent of us jerks live on two percent of the land."

"Can't be possible," I said.

"Check it out, homeboy," Koy said, using an un-Asian figure of speech. She was copying Zygolt. "We'll leave in a half-hour."

"Maybe you can teach me to do tricks," I said. "Give old Snowball a break."

Someone knocked on the front door.

"Just put the check under the mat!" Clytemnestra shouted.

"Excuse me," a woman's voice said from the other side of the door. "I'm looking for Max."

"The wife!" Clytemnestra hissed, grinning. "With the kids in a U-Haul trailer behind her."

"Who is it?" Zygolt shouted.

"FBI."

They jolted up. All looked at me.

"Don't go crazy," I said. "She's just a contact."

I pushed my chair back.

"That you, Merilee?" I shouted. "Or did you bring the SWAT team with you?"

"Just me. Can we please open this door?"

"Hold tight," I said, getting up. I got to the door and opened it.

Special Agent Merilee Combs was standing off-center to the door, like they train the recruits to do at the FBI Academy. Her left hand held the open credentials folder. Blue-green letters reading FBI were next to her serious snapshot on the card.

"Good to see that your jacket's open and that your right hand is free," I said. "There's no such thing as a routine visit."

"You're staying in the redneck quarter near the railroad tracks," she said. "The worst part of town. Why?"

"This is where the cab brought me from Amtrak. I'm no corporation, and the rent is cheap."

Today Merilee wore a charcoal gray business suit and a lightweight pink blouse with ruffles. Her shoes were glossy black and flat, with crepe soles for running.

The Showbizzers kept watching us.

"Is that the ex-wife?" Clytemnestra stage-whispered.

"Could be," Koy said.

"Or it could be The Other Woman," I said. "Keep an open mind."

"These are your roommates?" Merilee asked.

"Neighbors. My place is over there."

"Can we go there?" she asked.

Her voice surprised me. It had dropped down so that the Showbizzers could not hear it.

"Of course," I said. "But it's bachelor digs."

"I've seen them before."

☙

Her presence made my room feel shabby. Something had to be done about the butter-colored walls. Luckily, the open windows brought in the smell of the desert. Sunlight dappled the wall.

"All I have to offer you is tap water," I said. "Pretty foul."

"The NYPD has some pretty foul opinions about you, too," she said.

"Jealousy, just jealousy. They wish that they had my freedom. With a hardworking and dynamic FBI agent doing a home visit to see if I was really an ex-cop."

"'Mental Instability' was the official reason. And you swore that it was all job-related."

"Created by the Job, Special Agent. You know how it can happen. Look at your own agents committing suicide from stress. What do you have on Crosswaite?"

"I'm more interested in what we have on you."

"Can you tie him to the murder?" I asked.

"You know that I can't tell you anything like that. You're a civilian now. And what we call in the Bureau, 'a dis-organized person lacking candor'."

"Do you actually have such a term? WOOOF!"

"I schlepped out here to see your setup. What we are dealing with in you? Why are you in Basta again?"

"What kind of comely and arresting black woman uses the word 'schlepped?'"

"Well, why do you call me 'arresting?'"

"Because I'm sure that sometimes you are. Your job demands it."

"Enough word games, Mr. Royster. Why are you here again?"

"Just sitting out the winter with a bad leg. And maybe to fall in love with the girl next door."

"That wouldn't be me," she said. "Because you're involved in my case. I saw some of the girls next door at their breakfast table there."

"I can't fool the FBI."

"How's that love story going so far?"

"Are you going to be my big sister and confidante in this? That's sweet. So far, it isn't going."

"Maybe I'll check your story with the Sheriff's Department," she said.

"About falling in love?"

"No. About why you're here. They handle this part of Basta."

That was an unhappy thought. The deputies would tell her my Showbizzer idea. The FBI would not be pleased with me for that. They avoided volunteers.

"That's okay, then," I said. "But don't ask them about falling in love. They don't appear to be experts on that topics."

"Are you?"

"Is anybody?"

She cocked her head to one side.

"You know that we can't get a warrant on Crosswaite just because a couple of locals, with no names, said that one robber looked like Crosswaite. Basta is scared of him. Crosswaite reads a lot of history, according to my sources. He was fascinated with the Rebel guerrilla, Quantrill, who destroyed Lawrence, Kansas, during the Civil War. Crosswaite wanted to copy Quantrill and destroy Basta. But that's impossible with all our modern systems."

"No, it's not," I said. "Surprise still works. Blow up the power station after dark, destroy the police and sheriff's communications and blast a few gas-stations. Panic hits. Look at Seattle riots. New Orleans during Hurricane Katrina. Crosswaite could level this town and still get away clean."

"He's small-time," she said. "There was a deputy who bullied everyone on traffic stops. Crosswaite set him up and videotaped him stopping Crosswaite. Crosswaite took his abuse, recording it. Then he swarmed the deputy barehanded, put a wrestling hold on him and handcuffed him. Crosswaite stripped him naked and left him handcuffed to a billboard on the freeway. Then he broadcast it over the Internet. Some sided with Crosswaite. Everyone hates bully po-lice. The deputy resigned. That's Crosswaite's level. Not wrecking towns."

"I hear that the Basta cops are much better officers than the deputies are," I said.

Some amusement sparked in her eyes.

"No comment," she said.

"Dressed even more poorly than this," I said, "I pretended to be of humble origins and observed the deputies not protecting and not serving."

"Dressed worse than now?" she asked. "I'd like to see that sometime."

Merilee looked younger today than she had looked at the bank. Robbery-murder scenes aged everyone who worked them.

We considered each other.

She moved to the door and opened it deftly.

"I'll drop back from time to time to check on your wardrobe," she said. "And other things. Okay?"

"And you won't need a warrant."

After Merilee left, I waited outside for Koy, the woman next door.

❦

Koy appeared, looking more tense in her lean face. I tried talking but she scowled.

We walked in silence to her car.

On the way to the dog clients, I slouched in the back seat, alongside my crutches. I was getting used to this back seat. Snowball seemed to agree that I belonged there, too. He stuck his white head out the window and slopped his jowls against the black rubber on the frame. They were the same color as the rubber.

"I still think that what we're doing is sneaky," she said.

"Oh, showers of bastards. Can you just ask this dog family one question? Let's just say you trained a dog for the Crosswaite family. Then you got sick and could not train the dog anymore. So you owe them a refund. You want to pay them. They moved. Does anybody know where they are? That's all. Can you do that?"

"No, Max," she said. "Maybe Clytemnestra could do that. But I can't."

CHAPTER 18

Heartland

Looking at the desert, I thought of Koy's cancer.

"This Flowers family lives down Avenue K," Koy said.

"Avenue K?" I asked. "Just like Flatbush. But it sure looks different. Sand, tumbleweeds, scrubby grass and far-away mountains."

"They say that we drive fifteen minutes to reach their place. It's at the end of the road."

"That'll put us just about under that mountain there."

"Lot of desert rats build their homes in the shadow of a mountain. Afternoon sun can't hit it. The sun here can kill babies if it beats down on them long enough."

"Desolate," I said. "What were Lewis and Clark thinking when they came here?"

"Never did. They went north, through Montana and Idaho. Every fool who tried crossing this Mojave Desert died from heat, snakes or Native Americans. The Spanish explorers stuck to the California coast in their chain of mission churches."

"You really know these facts, Koy."

"Basta has plaques everywhere. This part of America stayed unknown except for prospectors until the 1920s. You must realize how new the West really is."

"And let me point out that we haven't seen a house here for the last five minutes. Those little bent-over trees and some buzzards in them."

"The Mormons tried colonizing around here. First whites to see those trees. They called them 'Joshua trees' because the trees reminded them of Joshua reaching his arms up to heaven."

"I know just how he felt," I said. "If I did that with my arms, something interior would tear and my crutches would drop and so would I."

"There's a house over there."

"It looks abandoned. Dried out. And there's another one. Looks empty, too."

We bounced along the dirt road. Snowball objected.

The golden mountain loomed high above us now. Shadows made charcoal strikes against the rock face. The road brought us to the base of the mountain. The air was still and smelled of something harsh and brackish, like overcooked fish.

"There's a house right up there against the mountain," Koy said.

☙

A small pink house with four or five cars scattered around it lay in front of us. Koy braked and parked inside a ranch-style fence. She made Snowball comfortable with the window half-open for his air.

The heat sapped me.

A burly, shirtless man came from behind the house. His right leg dragged behind him.

"You're the dog-trainer?" he called out.

"That's me," Koy said. "My name is Koy. Mr. Flowers?"

"Barrett Flowers," he said.

He looked her over. Koy might have been the first Chinese person he had seen outside of the Shanghai Delight Restaurant. Mr. Flowers did not appear to be a multicultural world citizen. Then he looked at me like I was a red-haired aging human trafficker in Asian flesh. He must have wondered just what kind of dog training he was getting.

A gaggle of white-blonde kids came out from the house. A liver-colored hound frolicked in the middle of them.

"You're the lady going to teach Rutherford?" the lankiest one asked. He was tanned a cocoa color by the sun, under blue eyes.

"I'll try," Koy said. The hound leaped at her. "This is Rutherford?"

"That goddamn sure is Rutherford," a woman coming out of the house said. Her blonde hair fell against cornflower blue eyes. Her body was perfectly round, with thick arms and work-scarred hands.

"Looks like a mud fence in a rainstorm," she said. "But he's all we got."

"Come on, Rutherford!" Koy said. Her face blossomed. She rubbed his neck. He jumped up on her leg.

"Let's see how well you can obey," she said.

Rutherford jumped up again and snapped at the air.

"If he could learn some tricks," Daddy Flowers said, "we could enter him in some shows and all. The kids would get a big kick out of that."

Daddy Flowers moved closer. He smelled like my running socks after my only marathon.

"Sure!" Koy bubbled. "Let's see what we can teach now."

For the next half hour, I watched Koy try to train Rutherford. It did not run smoothly. But Koy's looks captivated me, and it was fun to watch both of them. Country-Western guitar music spangled the air. Daddy Flowers sat and watched Koy, maybe ogling her as she tried to teach Rutherford how to heel.

"Rutherford Flowers," I said. "The Wonder Dog for our age."

"Mister, it's too damn hot out here," Daddy Flowers said.

"We need that icy air-conditioning like they got in Shooters Bar. Me and the boss here gonna go to their anniversary bash. Open bar. Would you like a beer or a ice drink?"

"Ice drink would be fine, thanks."

One of the kids brought me some sugary kind of lemon soda that I downed against the heat.

Mama Flowers paid Koy something for her time and gas. Zygolt would be pleased.

The kids kept pelting Koy with questions about Rutherford. They felt that Rutherford was headed straight for the big time in Las Vegas.

"I'll see about training him," Koy said. "First, I've got to square away my accounts around your area. I owe another family some money because I got sick and couldn't train their dog."

My head snapped up.

Koy was going through the story, just like I had asked. She had changed her mind about helping me.

"I'm driving around looking for them," Koy said. "Maybe you know them. Crosswaite."

"One Crosswaite guy stayed with Mrs. Santee," Mama Flowers said. "That must be thirty years ago. But they didn't have any dogs."

"Maybe they got them later," Koy said.

My face tried to stay bland. I concentrated on my sugary ice drink.

The family was petting and playing with Rutherford. Koy looked towards me.

My body tensed. I snapped fingers without making noise. It was time to roll the ex-cop universe into a ball towards The Big Question.

"Ma'am, do you know where Mrs. Santee is now?" I asked.

"Nossir, I sure don't."

I tried slowing down my Manhattan hurry-up speech tempo. It was better to take your time and get all folksy.

"Is there anybody who might kind of know where they are now?" I asked. "Because Koy here is running up a big gas bill trying to find them."

"Not that I can think of," Daddy Flowers said. "You're a good girl. You really want to find these people that bad just so you can pay them?"

Koy looked blank.

"She's religious," I said. "Some Chinese culture kind of thing. Honor and stuff. That's why they don't use credit cards and eat so many egg noodles. Where did they live?"

"Somewhere out in High Point. That's about six miles from here, off Fort Irwin Road where it hits Route 15."

Koy and I got back in with Snowball and said our good-byes to the Flowers and Rutherford.

"If you can train Rutherford, you can stretch bricks," I said.

"He's cute," she said.

"Cute? You are truly in love with your work," I said. "Thanks for asking about Crosswaite for me. If I had asked, they would not have opened up that much." "But they don't know much."

"It's a start," she replied. "Better than driving through the desert, shouting out 'Crosswaite, where are you?'"

Chapter 19

No Sleep

"Sleep is delicious," I remember saying in my sleep. "Delicious, delicious."

My thoughts lifted up and pulled me back in time. Tropical Mexico, sensual New Orleans and foggy San Francisco passed under my eyelids. My ex-wife rolled against my hip, murmured in her sleep and pinched my gut with her elbow.

Police radios cackled.

Just like in daylight life, I tried ignoring them.

They kept jabbering.

"Delicious sleep ain't so delicious any more," I whispered. "Cops!"

My feet tangled in the sheet. The left knee sang songs of pain and loss.

"James Bond springing into action like a tiger," I muttered.

Red lights waltzed through my butter-colored room. They reflected in the tiny mirror.

This was real life.

Cop cars were outside my room, with their red lights revolving and radios burping.

"Police Commissioner's revenge," I said to myself. "He sent cops to bag me for something or other."

Scooping up my new wallet with my temporary ID, I threw on a pair of cut-offs and a T-shirt. Back in New York,

Internal Affairs would come after bad cops like this in the middle of the night for shock value, to rock the cop's family as hard as possible. Images of Central Booking and the dirty-feet smell of the inmates swarmed back.

Then my head cleared.

"Hey, Commissioner," I said. "I haven't done anything wrong. So keep it in your pants."

Relieved, I sank down on my head. The fear-sweat oozing from me dried up. So I would not have to run through the swamps with bloodhounds bating after me. There would be no manhunt. No mud would ooze between my fingers.

"Open up!" someone young shouted outside. "County sheriffs!"

"They're not at my door," I said. "Not yet, anyway."

"Open this door," the same young voice said. "Or else we'll boot it in and arrest everyone inside for Obstruction!"

"Mister subtle," I muttered. "My Showbizzer kids are going to need some finesse with this idiot."

Not bothering with my contact lenses, I speared my cherry-red eyeglasses and put them on. Shower flip-flops completed the look.

My thrift shop wrist-watch said that it was just past six.

Turning on all my two lights – doorway and living room, I stepped out onto the ground, keeping my hands high and visible. Otherwise, some jittery deputy might get rude with me and make noise.

Three San Risa Sheriff's cars parked in the dirt space between my room and the Showbizzers' house. Deputies in their tan khakis were bunched up in front of the door. That proved their bad tactics once again. One shooter could take them all out in a quick burst.

No lights showed in the Showbizzers' house.

Dawn was streaking the sky.

"Excuse me, deputies," I said.

Either they did not hear me or they chose to ignore me. Take your choice.

"Police!" I shouted.

Sometimes you have to shout. With badge-heavy dolts, you have to clamor.

Now, they turned. I hobbled over near them.

One unit had the door open. Hip-hop music came from a portable radio on the unit's front seat. It grated on my ears.

"I'm glad that you react to that word 'police!'" I said. "Heard it before, have you?"

"You're saying that you're police, right?" one with a Zapata moustache said.

They tensed.

"No, no," I said. "I was just calling out to you. Giving you a shout-out, like the kids say."

"We're not police, we're deputies," Zapata said.

"There's a lot in that one sentence," I said.

"Mister," another deputy, looking as wide as a barrel with bangs of black hair on his forehead, said. "You live here? You got any ID or just come out here to pass smart remarks?"

"It's six in the morning," I said.

"Yeah, that means that it's just about time for you to shut up and go to bed," Zapata said without taking a deep breath.

"Maybe I can help you," I said.

"Listen, stupid," Zapata said.

"I know," I said. "You just told me how."

"How what?" Wide-As-A-Barrel said.

"How can I help you? You just told me 'Time for you to shut up and go to bed.' But I can help you. Teach you some charm."

"Got your badge?" came the routine question.

"Got robbed of all my ID and cash my first night in your fair city. To be fair to you guys, it was county land where the sheriff was supposed to protect me."

As I had hoped, someone moved inside the Showbizzer home. Maybe they were flushing drugs.

"What in the Sam Hill is 'Detached Service'?" Zapata said. "Sounds like you're selling us some snake oil, mister."

"Special designation of highly select officers, attached to the Commissioner's office," I said.

That was true enough. The last time that the Commissioner had spoken to me, he had promised to build a special place for me and never let me out.

It was all in the wording.

"We got a warrant for a Murline Sparks," Zapata said. "Simple battery."

"Step aside or we'll lock you up right now," Barrel said.

I bet that he was quoting a line from TV to his new audience.

"Step aside? I'm ten feet behind you in my flip-flops. Go do what you want."

They gave off a group exhale and turned back to the house.

"Except maybe one thing," I said.

They blew out breaths again and turned back to me. All of them carried big black Maglite flashlights. They toyed with them, tapping them against their forearms.

"I spent more years in uniform than you could ever believe," I said. In truth, I had not served for long, with my suspensions.

"It shows," Barrel said. He was the shrewd one in this group of bully-beef boys.

"Maybe, cop-to-cop, you guys maybe could go get coffee first and then go serve this warrant," I said.

"Say that again and we'll lock you up right now."

My toes ground in the flip-flops. They were insulting me. Civilians could never understand just how that insult cut.

"Slugging you would just kill my experiment," I muttered.

"Huh?"

"Nothing, deputy."

I was trying to waste their time until my Showbizzers could protect themselves. Patrol cops wasted oceans of time every day.

A door opened in the building to the left. The deputies tensed. Their hands went to their hip holsters and nudged their semiauto pistols.

Chick, the owner, came out in his bathrobe and glasses on. He saw the deputies and stopped short.

"That's the landlord," I said. "And I am real glad to see him. He'll fix this."

"Who are you, mister?" Barrel asked Chick.

Chick tried to smile. He never spoke much. At first, I thought that he was just the desk clerk here, renting rooms by the day, week or month. But Marcus had said that he owned the entire spread of 26 rooms and three buildings and the land.

"You fellas all know me," he said. "I'm Chick Swarton. You are always welcome here, you know that."

"Get back in your room or we'll arrest you for Interference," Zapata said, deadpan.

Chick's face fell apart. He pivoted and went back to his room fast. His slippers clacked.

"Hey, I was just kidding!" Zapata said. "Yo! Chick! Jesus."

"Guy's too sensitive," another deputy said from the shadows. He was too far back to see.

"That kind of kidding really helps your reputation," I said. "Look at that sad, scared loser Chick. I'll never understand people."

The lights went out in Chick's house. Maybe he was hiding under the covers.

"Let's get back to work," Barrel said.

Zapata pounded on the front door with his Maglite flashlight.

"Murline Sparks!" he shouted. "Open up! Sheriff's deputies with a warrant!"

"I'm opening this door," Zygolt's voice said. "There is nobody here with that name. Sure not me. Do I look like a Murline Sparks to you?"

She opened the door, wearing a towel wrapped around her. The claret-colored bathrobe must be hanging up somewhere else.

"What do you want?" she asked. "You wake us up in the middle of the night."

"Warrant like this is good anytime after six," Barrel said. "And you lower your voice, or I'll case you myself and put you in the car."

"'Case you?' And what does that mean, pray tell?" I asked.

"It means arrest you," another deputy said, with sunglasses folded over his shoulder epaulets. Maybe he was primed for a blazing sunrise. "Are you sure that you're a police?"

"Not like you are."

"There's nobody here by that name," Zygolt said.

"You're a liar," Sunglasses said.

"Get out of here," Zygolt said. Her voice climbed. "Do it. Or I'll call the real police. The Basta police."

"This is not their territory," Barrel said.

"That's right," I said. "Their territory starts at the back of the Desert Market. Or is it the front of the Desert Market?"

"Basta Police can't do anything," Sunglasses said.

"Maybe not," I said. "But you never tell that to a civilian."

"We the real police, waddy."

"Dear me," I said. "Dear, dear me."

"This Sparks air-head," Barrel said. "Got red hair and is real skinny. Bad temper."

Zygolt and I looked over the deputies at each other.

"Clytemnestra!" I said.

"Ma'am, we all know that she's in there. Gave this address to the arresting deputies. Now we got to bring her to Alcohol De-Tox."

"Either she comes out or we boot this door in and take her," Zapata said.

"I'm sorry that I slammed you before," Zygolt said. "I know that in this part of the city, you are the real police. But why do some call you 'Sheriff's Department' and others call you 'Sheriff's Office'?"

"Calling us 'Sheriff's Office' is old-timey," Zapata said. "Basta likes old-timey. Is she coming out or do we do this the hard way?"

"Clytemnestra!"

"I'm coming," Clytemnestra said. "I was just packing. Toothbrush and stuff. Hi, Deputy Morse! You were the one who busted me, right?"

"That's right, Miss Sparks," Sunglasses said. "You were slap-ass drunk. I'm surprised that you remember."

"I remember anyone that I need to remember," she giggled.

Zygolt and I looked at each other and shook our heads. Marcus came out, wearing heavy eyeglasses. He must use contact lenses during the day, like me. Koy crowded behind him in a Kelly green bathrobe with some cream on her skin. Snowball gazed at all of us and yawned.

"This doesn't bother you?" Zygolt asked Clytemnestra. "Going to jail?"

"It's just De-Tox," Clytemnestra said. "I've been through it before."

"Clytemnestra," I said, "your real name is Murline Sparks? But you told me that your hippie parents had named you Clytemnestra. Which is it?"

"Oh, you know," Clytemnestra said.

I blew out a breath and rocked back on my crutches.

"These kids today, I tell you," I repeated.

It was a line that my Showbizzers were forcing me to use a lot.

"See you guys soon!" Clytemnestra hollered.

Sunglasses handcuffed her and led her to his cruiser.

The deputies shut off the red lights and drove off the property.

"Those attracted to acting," I muttered, "often had unsatisfactory personal lives to begin with. Someone once wrote a book about that."

The remaining Showbizzers looked at me.

"When in doubt, go back to sleep," I said. "Watch me do it."

They gaped at me.

"Appearing callous never appeals to me," I said. "But losing sleep won't help Clytemnestra, née Murline. If she needs help. She acts like a joyous tyke bounding off to summer camp."

ও

My hardish cheap bed felt good to me.

The sun was cooking my room again by the time that I woke up.

Going outside groggy, I smelled coffee and bacon from the house and knocked on the door.

"More deputies?" Zygolt's voice came out.

"Just Max."

"Come in. We can nuke breakfast up again for you," she said.

Snowball lay near the kitchen in his favorite spot. I threw my cash into the jar marked "Tips for Artists" like I did every day.

Koy and Zygolt sat at the table.

"Marcus is off a-banking at his job and hopefully learning more about the robbery," I said.

"So far, he had gotten nothing new," Koy said.

"Undercover like that takes time," I replied.

"But he said that they have accepted him and like his acting stories."

"When he wants to be, Marcus is a damn good charmer," Zygolt said. "Probably got tellers in love with him already."

"Something will break," I said. "You'll see. Koy, can you and I go to High Point today looking for the lost Crosswaite-Santee clan?"

"Absolutely not," Koy said. "I asked your stupid question for you. That's it. No more. Finished. A lay is a play."

"'A lay is a play'," I quoted her. "I'm sure learning lots of new expressions from you Showbizzers. What does that charming expression mean?"

"I don't know. My father used to say it. Even though his English is way rotten. It probably means 'enough is enough.'"

"Sounds like an expression from a house of ill repute," I said. "Meaning that once joy has been achieved, then the action must cease until more moneys are paid. Captivating turn of phrase."

"So I'm not going," she said. "Period. That's final."

"A lay is a play," I said. "Koy, I'll just say this once. You and I started looking for Crosswaite. You're Chinese, and I am a rapidly aging redhead. Bastas notice us. Our cover story is that you owe Crosswaite money."

"I know all this. It's getting to be a bore."

"If I start looking alone, desert rats who heard our cover story will wonder where you are. They may suspect me as a cop and blow me up."

"Then don't go. Forget the whole cuckoo idea."

On purpose, my head did not turn to Zygolt. If she did not use her authority, as Showbizzer Big Mama, to request Koy to do this, then my asking Zygolt would not help. So I did not ask.

"All right, Koy," I said.

Hopefully, my voice did not show my anger right now.

A skilled negotiator would advise me to drop the request now. So I concentrated on breakfast. Everything went better with a full belly.

"This is like asking one woman to dance," I said. "She declines. So you ask a different woman at the same table. Zygolt, would you care to dance with me out to High Point today? A man and a woman are a couple, just helping out Koy. If I go out alone, locals may see me as a cop."

"No, I would not," Zygolt said. "We used to have the four of us working together to make a living in Basta. Like everyone else, we need money to eat and stay warm at night. But because of you, Clytemnestra is locked down. Marcus is getting all screwed up and losing focus for acting in some banking gig."

"Wouldn't worry about that. He seems to hate the job nicely enough."

"So why should I risk everything to go hunting with you?"

A laptop computer lay on the kitchen counter. I limped over, tapped some keys and pressed the print button.

"Here's why, Zygolt," I said. "The American Bankers Association put this out on their website. They're offering thirty-thousand dollars for anyone who gives information and gets the bank robbers arrested. Not even convicted. Just arrested. Would that 30K help you out here?"

"You know it would. But we can't get it."

"Seeing how the deputies and the cops operate in this town, I think that you could. You've looked them over. With your brains, discipline and skill, don't you feel that you can out-think them and find Crosswaite?"

"How about you just scooping up the reward and leaving us in the lurch?"

"When we get him, we split the reward five ways," I said. "Clytemnestra helped, in her way."

"Her way," Koy said. "Zygolt, you need real protection. Like Snowball. So take Snowball. He can protect you better than Max."

Both women scrutinized me. Maybe they were remembering other men and other broken promises.

"Zygolt, if you want, we can stop off at a lawyer's office and draw up a contract that way," I said. "Just so that it's legal. A five-way split."

"You've got a shotgun, right?" Zygolt said. "Bring it today and I'll come. With Snowball. Thanks, Koy. Just for today."

"Just for today, I will. It's a deal. We'll leave whenever you want. But we have to learn how to work without relying on a gun. To cajole and convince others to give us information. When you can do that, you have real power."

"All power comes out of the barrel of a tongue," Koy said. "Isn't that what Chairman Mao Tse-tung said? More or less."

"Bad translation from the Mandarin," I said. "Sure. Have your fun. But remember that's what wrong with our deputies. And cops in general. They rely too much on their authority and their gun. They don't try outthinking the perps."

Chapter 20

Into the Wild

"Zygolt, why did you make your appearance before those deputies half-naked in a towel?" I asked.

We bumped out over the railroad bridge and into the desert.

She turned the Roadmaster wheel and her bright smile lit her face again.

"It's your jacked-up training," she said.

"My training? I taught you to get naked in front of lusty, hairy-legged deputies?"

"You preached us, the quickest way to derail a cop raid was to threaten them with an internal complaint."

"And I ought to know," I said.

"So everyone knows that you cops are sex-obsessed. Need mothering. Spanking."

"Well," I said.

"So I nailed it down in my noggin that I had sex available. Albeit old sex."

"You'll never be old," I said.

"So, if necessary, I would have bumped into a deputy or two, let the towel fall and start screaming. Mucho distraction, brother."

"That's me. I'm Big Brother, watching over all my kids."

"Very different world you live in, Max."

"Not so very. Three or four professional dancers I know joined the Job. Don't forget that it is also physical work, using your body outdoors. I used to call street policing 'The Concrete Ballet'."

"'The Concrete Ballet', huh?"

"Zygolt, I'm dying to hear the story of your life."

"As a kid, I liked to skip everywhere that I went. Could fly way up high and hang in the air that way. Dancing gave me that same feeling."

"When did you start?"

"Must have been way young. 'cause I don't remember my first class. There was a county pool near Eugene, Oregon, that had a high diving board. Scared me and exhilarated me at the same time. Every day, I walked up that ladder, looked out and froze. Could not jump into the water that was only about twelve feet under me."

"When you're a child, twelve feet looks enormous," I said.

"All blankety-blank summer! One day, I went up there and just stepped off the board. I was flying! Rushing through the air. After that, I jumped off that board every day that Jesus sent."

"For nights afterwards, I dreamed of flying as I slept. Had something in common with the comic book superheroes. Dancing is still like flying to me."

"Did you dance in school?"

"As much as I could. Cheerleader, too. Everything with dance. Then took it at San Francisco State. Danced in show-cases of *West Side Story*, your city. *Carousel, Hair*. Some that I need therapy to forget. *Morisannia Coringo Follies, Sueno, Rocky Jones, Space Ranger* and some other flat-out disasters. I kept learning new steps and new styles. The world of dance has no bottom to it."

℃

We had left the Flowers' family mountain behind us. The desert swallowed me up again, making me feel like a fly on a football field.

"What is your favorite dancing role?" I asked.

"Anita in *West Side Story*. In my view, the finest American musical ever written. Audiences love *Showboat* or *Porgy and Bess*, but nothing is so solid as *West Side Story*. Every line is inspired."

"In between gigs?"

"Teaching dance in public schools. Turns into combat sometimes. The usual waitress routine. Office temp. You were never in a place long enough to learn the job. Married twice and wound up supporting both of them. I must look like a gullible fool. One was a dancer like me. He was always about to do something or other."

"Most dancers could not keep up that life," I said. "They would marry and start a scrapbook of their best shows. And look back with regret."

"There are two kinds of artists, Max. The kind who stop. And the kind who continue. There is no third kind."

"Continue to do what?"

"To do whatever is different. That is art. Walking is just walking until you do it differently and it blooms into dance."

More golden sand encircled us.

A dark clump crouched on the horizon. We got closer. A church steeple sharped against the deep blue sky.

"According to AAA maps, that should be High Point right there," I said.

"Hope you're sure. Some of these paved roads go on for miles and miles without any houses. Then the pavement changes to a dirt road. And then the dirt road ends. Sometimes at the county line. And you gotta drive all the way back."

"That feels dangerous to this New Yorker," I said. "Bikers with assault rifles, right-wing militia Ritz Crackers or crazed druggies like the Manson Family that they never caught."

"That's right. Some got away."

"Maybe they came here and raised murderous children," I said. "Luckily, Snowball is our protection. Koy says that he's attack-trained."

"Even trained him to respond to my voice," Zygolt said. "To protect the house. Basta scares everyone."

∾

The houses got bigger as we neared them. The gray stone steeple dominated the cluster of dried wood shacks and stucco buildings. Six or seven mobile homes lay at different places near the crossroads.

An adobe sign read "High Point."

There was nothing more.

Nobody was anywhere here. I looked for movement and saw none.

She pulled up near the church.

"Do you see anyone?" she asked.

"No registered voters here," I said.

For some reason, we were whispering.

"Let Snowball out," I said. "I don't like this a bit."

The morning wind riffled through the buildings. A dry goods store and gas station with dead metal pumps stood like monuments to the California highway epic. A Coca-Cola sign from the Kennedy administration lay cracked near the pumps.

Snowball unrolled, looking blasé as usual. He sniffed and poked but found nothing appetizing.

We moved around the side of the church.

Nothing stirred except the wind.

Broken glass hung in all the windows.

Some local with a scattergun might hear us and take action.

"Hello!" I tried shouting in a bluff, hearty and manly voice like John Wayne. "Anybody here?"

There was.

Wild pigs rushed us from behind the church. One slammed into my crutch and spun me around.

They ganged us. They butted into me again. Tusks flashed. They grunted. Zygolt kicked one away. Others hit her.

"They can kill you!" Zygolt shouted.

Greasy matted hair covered them. The sharp tusks came up as high as my leg artery.

"Get Snowball!" I shouted.

"Snowball!" Zygolt shouted. "Attack!"

Snowball attacked. He leaped at one pig. They were the same size. The pig was thicker. About eight others nipped at Snowball. They grunted loud.

Zygolt kicked out, spun around and got her legs bent under her. She crouched and then sprang up high onto an abandoned stove by the church wall. Pigs ran into the stove. It rocked.

"Attack! Attack!" Zygolt shouted.

Snowball turned and ran. Pigs whipped their tusked heads at him. I swung my left crutch and hit one in the head. Their skin looked tough everywhere. They smelled of mud and dead things.

The Academy on East 20th Street never taught us anything about handling wild boars.

"Snowball!" Zygolt shouted. "Come back here!"

Snowball was not having any of it. He had charged once and that was it for the day. Shop closed, boss. He go home.

He used his training to get to our car, jump up on the hood and watch us.

One pig caught my jeans leg. His tusks worked.

CHAPTER 21

After the Pigs

A metal stove burner spun through the air. It hit my pig on the snout. The filthy fly-specked metal bounced off his snout. It hit his buddy pig's face.

The burner was the size of my hand.

From atop the stove, Zygolt pried up another and winged it at a third pig behind the first two. Her jeans were ripped like mine where the pigs had struck her.

My crutches saved me. The pigs kept bumping into the wood. Maybe they could not see well. Tusks scraped the wood.

"Max! Get over here!"

Pigs kept getting in the way. Maybe they were stupid. They ran grunting into each other.

Swinging crutches, I got to Zygolt's stove. My back against it so they could not ambush me, I kept kicking with my good leg.

A green Jeep roared up from the road and drove through the herd. A horn honked. The Jeep nailed one pig against the church wall. The pig dropped.

The Jeep backed up and hit some more pigs. The driver hit the horn again.

The pigs broke and scattered.

They ran rooting back behind the church.

They vanished.

"Max, did they gore you?"

"They tried."

"They're killers!"

"So you said."

"Those javelinas got a bad attitude," the Jeep driver said. "They will jump you like that for no reason."

He was a compact wood-chip of a man, with a smallish gray moustache and hair cut short. His nervous eyes darted over both of us.

"Thank you," I said. "We owe you a lot."

"The Lord says for us to help our neighbor when his ox or ass falls into a ditch," he said. "They keep trying to talk away the Word but they just can't."

"I was terrified," I said. That was no lie. "One of those tusks hits your artery, and all your troubles are over."

"Yes," he said. "The Hereafter."

"Snowball!" Zygolt called. "Get off that car and come here! Heel!"

Snowball stayed right where he was. His body said that there might be hidden pigs lurking under the Roadmaster's chassis. So he was staying right where he was.

Zygolt walked over to him and went around the back of the car. A clump of Joshua trees stood nearby. I reached down and picked up a sharp-edged tree branch about six inches long.

My right jeans leg was torn across the thigh. The gash in the jeans gaped. I put the branch's point against my own skin and ran it back and forth. There was not much time.

The branch scratched and scraped and finally broke the skin. There was a scratch as long as my index finger visible through the torn jeans.

"Come here, warrior hound," I told Snowball.

He was not leaving the hood of the car. I left him there, still protecting himself.

"That's an interesting attack dog we got there," I said, limping back. "Maybe you and Koy better re-train him somewhat."

Our rescuer still sat in his Jeep. He saw no reason to move. He was kind of like Snowball.

"I'm Max Royster," I said, reaching through the window.

"Tom Morris," he said, taking my hand in his soft one.

"We called out to people living here," I said. "But it was no go."

"Oh, nobody lives here. No, take that back. It's kind of hard to tell. Some drift back and sleep in the ruins." He pronounced it 'roons'. "Desert rats, you know, they're funny."

"Hilarious," I said.

Zygolt looked past my crutches at my leg.

"Max, you got cut?" she asked.

I reached down with my hand and opened up the blue jeans gash.

"Yup, I guess the hogs got me after all," I said. "Broke the skin anyway. And look at my crutches. All nicked up and stuff. They stopped the hogs from getting more of my skin. They kept bumping into each other like they were blind."

"Half-blind, yeah," Morris said. "Good smell and vicious as you now know but they can't see. That scratch could infect. Those javelinas are filthy creatures."

"Yeah, it could infect," I said. "Because of the pain-killers that I'm taking for the knee, I'm in a delicate stage."

That was a lie. I watched Morris.

"Yeah, you don't want that infected," he said. "You got a first-aid kit in that car?"

"We've got flyers for my dance school."

"Dance school?" Morris said. "That's no good. You should always keep a first-aid kit in your car."

We fell silent, wondering why Morris did not have a kit in his car.

"Okay," Morris said. "Follow me in your rig and I'll get that scrape fixed up at my place. You don't want to go to Valley General in Victorville. Full of Mexicans. Don't like to take you out of your way."

"That's okay," I said. I wondered what he was talking about.

He seemed to make his mind up about something. "Okay," he said. "Just follow me."

We coaxed Snowball-The-Wonder-Dog off our hood and followed Tom Morris down the two-lane county road.

"When we moved here, they warned us how dangerous those javelina hogs can be," Zygolt said. "But none of us go mucking about in the desert." She glanced at me. "Except when you push us to it."

"Sure. Blame me. All my fault. The pigs are in my pay. 'Mucking about', you did say?"

"One of my husbands was a Scot," she said. "Supposed to even be royalty. With a castle. I never saw it."

"Sorry for waking up the memories."

"It's a place where I don't go much anymore. I got anti-depressants for his memory."

We kept following Morris.

"Do you think that he's a crazed high desert killer?" she asked.

"The 'high desert'?" I asked.

"That's just what they call this place."

"He's high on something. Maybe himself. Maybe that Lord guy that he mentioned."

Mountains passed on both sides.

Fat clouds threw shadows across acres of desert.

"Come on, Morris," I said. "This is growing arduous."

"Are you hurting, boss man?" she asked.

"Those crushing boars rattled me good. Again and again, I wonder how I ever lasted in this business."

"Because you're tough?"

"Ha!"

A housing development with an earthen wall around it drew closer. A burnt wood sign announced "Wagon Wheel Apartments."

Morris drove into the entrance and spoke to the blue-shirted security guard in his booth. Morris pointed at us.

"There's my next job," I said.

"Why do they have a development this far out?" Zygolt asked. "And why a security guard in nowhere? This is way wombat."

"Tenants want to be in the desert but not really in the desert," I said. "And the toy cop out front makes them feel safer from those marauders that we spoke of. Or maybe from those packs of wild little piggie-wiggies."

We followed him down rows of identical adobe-style condominiums. Signs outside some announced "Condos! Condos! Condos!"

"Come to the New American West!" I said. "You expect to find a grizzled prospector like Gabby Hayes with his faithful mule Nellybelle panning for gold in the creek. Dodging Apache arrows. Instead we are treated to this."

Morris stopped at a condo driveway and pointed to the flagstone sidewalk where Zygolt should park.

He used a key ring device to unlock the condo's front door. My knees bent and my hands went up as I followed him inside. Today had enough surprises already. The wild boars had truly rattled me.

Pictures of angels and saints filled his walls. Maybe he took his strength from them. He was a gutsy guy to break up the pig fest and then bring us to his home.

"Head into the bedroom and drop those jeans," he said. "I'll get some cure-all kind of stuff that I picked up. Unless your wife wants to put it on herself."

"Enough troubles in my life without being his wife," Zygolt said.

"We're not even sweethearts," I said. "Or likely to be. We're out here doing a favor for a friend."

"That so?"

Morris' gray eyebrows climbed.

Inside his religiously painted bedroom, I fed him my cock-and-bull story about looking for Crosswaite-Santee.

Meanwhile, I painted my thigh with his cure-all.

"Tom, what's in this ointment?" I asked. "This label tells me nothing. It could be old stump-remover, for all of me."

"Good stuff," he said.

"I'm asking you about this Crosswaite family because I figure that you're old family around this desert."

"Oh, no! I'm from Ohio. Hated the winters there."

I stopped painting my skin. It felt like someone had put a torch underneath it and forgotten to turn it off.

Koy was right. Giving him my Crosswaite cover story did feel slimy. But Crosswaite might kill again.

"How long have you been out here, Tom?" I asked.

"Forty-two years. Thank the Lord and His plan."

"Yeah. So you heard about this Crosswaite-Santee family?"

He paused. My eyes turned to him.

"Gossip is abhorrent to what I hold with," he said.

This was going to be a mud-and-adobe wall made in heaven.

"Yes, but 'Do you see a man diligent in his business? He shall stand before kings.'"

His eyes locked on mine.

"And," I said. "'The laborer is worthy of his hire.'"

"But she owes them money."

"It goes double when it is the other way around," I said. "Everyone knows that."

"Oh?" he said.

In his bedroom, I did not want to rupture the just-us-boys-together atmosphere.

"Where can I give this Crosswaite family their money?" I asked. "They could use it, I'm sure."

"Not Sam Crosswaite. He's with the Lord now," he said. "From my mission work here, I knew every family.

"You're wanting to speak to Wayne, his son. Wayne grew up with the Santee woman taking care of him. That was more than 25 years ago. He was an only child. God knows where he lives now."

"What was Mrs. Santee's first name?" I asked.

He made a face of agony.

"Blessed if I can remember it right now."

The front door opened. I felt vulnerable. My jeans went up to my hips again. A woman's voice spoke with Zygolt.

"It's alright, Barbie!" Morris called out. "They're just new friends who had some bad luck."

He opened the bedroom.

A black woman, slim and statuesque, came through the front door. Her black hair was piled in a style that made her look even taller. Her ebony skin showed no signs of wear but she was about the same age as Morris. Her teeth parted in a smile of welcome. She had the grace of an actress. Clytemnestra could learn from her.

"Come to my house and be happy," she said in a lilting accent. "Tom, you don't offer her anything? They will think that we are African barbarians!"

She threw back her head and laughed.

"Dear, they were just asking about the Crosswaite family," Morris said. "I'm trying but I can't remember that woman's first name."

"Elsa," the woman that he called Barbie said. "Mrs. Santee's first name was Elsa."

"That's right. And she saw that doctor all the time for imaginary illnesses."

"That was Dr. Spratt," Barbie said. "In Victorville. If he is still practicing."

"I wish that the Lord had given me your memory, dear," Morris said.

"You've both lived here a long time," I said, feeling not very bright. Again.

"Like I said, 42 years," Morris said. "Ever since I came back from the mission in Kenya."

"When Sam died, I wonder what Elsa did with all his stuff," Morris said.

"What kind of stuff?" I asked.

"He was a gun collector. He had lots of them. They're probably still in the family."

Chapter 22

I Am the Wine Buyer

"Tonight, I'm the wine buyer," I said as the sun was setting over Route 66 Arms. "Time for a slap-up good dinner."

"What's the occasion?" Koy asked.

She tapped me on the shoulder and let her hand stay there.

Her touch warmed me. It felt like high school again.

"Boredom," I said. "What the French call *ennui*. Germans name it *weltschmerz*. No good for you. Life is good. We should eat and drink that way."

"That may be impossible in Basta. What's the best restaurant here?"

"Silver Saddle Steakhouse," Zygolt said.

"Let's get them on the phone," I said. "We need something to match this."

The Showbizzers looked over at me.

A case of Côtes du Rhone wine lay inside my duffle bag.

"If I drink enough of this tonight, I'll take the bandage off my leg," I said. "According to what the sawbones in Manhattan told me, four weeks is enough time for the healing. Now I can walk on a cane."

"Do you even have a cane?" Marcus asked.

"You better take me shopping."

"I got some loose talk from the bank that you are going to love!" he said, eyes glowing.

My gut swelled out. Maybe my Showbizzer plans would work.

"Good work!" I said.

"This teller was gabbing –"

"Keep it until after dessert," I said. "Did you write it down first?"

"Just like you trained us. And the ladies at the bank like the way I dress."

"They probably like it more the way you undress," Zygolt said.

"Do you know what one calls me?"

"I can't imagine."

Marcus beamed, hugged himself, jumped up and drummed his feet on the floor.

"Dapper!" he shouted.

An hour later, we were biting into prime rib steaks, garlic roasted potatoes, creamed spinach, Brussels sprouts and tomato bruschetta. The red wine washed it down wonderfully.

Guitar folk music flowed out of the music system.

"This feels so right," Marcus said. "We don't get too many chances to enjoy food like this. I've been researching. Do you know that up until the 1930s, some states did not recognize an actor's marriage? Or allow him to leave property to his kids?"

"Why not?"

"Because us actors were considered outside the Common Law. Not real members of society. Weird freaks living on lust and liquor and pretending to be other people."

"Do you have this much cash to fling around?" Zygolt asked.

"Sometimes the bill is worth it, no matter how high it is," I said. "The wine buyer will not be denied."

Koy's cheeks reddened. Liquor sometimes pinked up Asian skin. She laughed more and played with Snowball who was addressing himself to a steak bone under the table.

"Have old-fashioned rice pudding with cinnamon or crème brulée for dessert," Zygolt said. "If any of you crime fighters has room for it."

My gut had that happy solid feeling that came after a tasty steak.

"Just what you've been waiting for," I said. "I'm the wine buyer."

"You keep saying that," Koy said.

"What does all that mess mean?" Marcus said.

"You'll find out. It's my way of seducing all of you." The wine was twirling my head. "Marcus, say what you got and we'll figure a way to use it."

"Oh, teacher, now?" Zygolt groaned. "That's just like homework."

Marcus beamed and acted as though he was on center stage on Broadway. With a flourish, he took out a thick brown cigar and lit it with a wooden kitchen match. The aroma filled the dining room.

"I'm helping out another teller when we got real busy," Marcus said. "And an old regular customer named Roger Alicea is on the customer line. Chatters about a woman named Gretchen raising horses here. Gretchen sometimes hears automatic weapons shooting off on her spread at night. She rode out in daylight. Found heaps of shell casings."

"Great work, Dapper Marcus," I said. "Now, including me, we are all in training. Who knows what we need now?"

Holding dessert plates and wineglasses, they looked back at me.

"Dig, Showbizzers, dig," I said. "This is what it means to be the wine buyer. Pay for an exquisite meal and then everyone brainstorms and talks about our current case. We all compare notes. Drum up new ideas."

"So it's like a screenwriting story session?" Marcus said.

"You're the artist. You tell me."

"Max, this is San Risa County," Koy said.

"Do you know why the gringos named it 'San Risa County'" Marcus asked. "First settlers here were dying of thirst. But this here Indian woman who spoke zip English but had a beautiful smile saved their lives by leading them to water. Then the cavalry killed her trying to force her people to evacuate. In Spanish, *risa* means 'smile'. In her honor, they named this county after her."

"They would not name it after a non-white woman today," Koy said. "There is too much racism. My parents warned me about it. It has more reported right-wing militia groups than anywhere in the States. They want to protect America against us Asians. Could be the ones shooting at night. It does not have to be our suspects."

"Our 'clients'," I corrected her. "Or call them 'subjects', please."

"Why call these killers 'clients'?" Marcus asked.

"We try to do that because it is a neutral and non-judgmental way of naming them. It does not imply that we are better than they are."

"But we are!" Zygolt said, tilting her eighth or ninth glass of wine. She looked childish and carefree now, under the years. "They are killers."

"But in court, their defense lawyer may ask how you referred to them," I said. "If you call them 'scum', 'bad guys', 'mutts' or 'perps', the defense lawyer may say that you were already prejudiced against them from the start. So stay neutral. It wins the hearts of jurors."

"Big Daddy Max," Marcus said. "I hear you call them 'perps' sometimes."

"As gently as possible, Showbizzers," I said, "I must tell you that your Big Daddy Max is not always a perfect creature."

"We've noticed," Koy said.

"If we ever get to court," I said, "you want the machinery and the jury to see you as an average person. Not an avenging angel or a vigilante. Crime disturbs you, you use your wits to give your ideas and information to the police and you do not involve your emotions in it."

"Juries will believe that?"

"Juries can be pretty thick sometimes," I said. "I remember one time when they convicted the judge."

"They will know that we want the reward," Koy said.

"If we're lucky, there will be no trial and no mention of a reward," I said. "Maybe I'm wandering far afield here. But we cannot work if locals are afraid to talk to us."

"What do you mean?"

"Explain that," Koy said. "Totally, I mean. Don't leave anything out."

"When they first formed the FBI in 1908, the Bureau did not want America too scared to talk to them," I said. "You want the entire speech? Traditionally, Americans mistrust any kind of secret police. So they came up with a strategy."

"Which was?"

"The Bureau looked at the institutions that America trusted. Not the police. At that time, they were corrupt, non-effective and brutal. The Army? Too much militarism and recent blood on their hands from the Philippines. But we respected the railroads. They had changed the world since their invention, less than a hundred years before. Railroads settled the West."

"In towns like Basta," Koy said.

"Yep. Citizens trusted the railroads with their lives, luggage and children. Folks who hated blacks would trust their kid to a smiling black Pullman porter who would show his teeth and shout 'Yassuh!' for a tip."

"So the Bureau adapted railroad terms for itself. There were no military ranks. The titles were 'Supervisor' or 'Night Supervisor' or 'Agent.' Nice friendly titles. Nothing bloody or soldierly about them. The Bureau wanted America's trust first. For legal reasons, they had to add the word 'Special' in front of 'Agent.' But they stressed a frank and friendly approach to everything, not to frighten anyone."

"That was Hoover?"

"J. Edgar Hoover was thirteen years old when the Bureau was founded. I doubt that he had much to do with their shaping the image."

Marcus leaped to his feet and smiled his wicked, wolf-like smile.

"J. Edgar Hoover was," Marcus said, searching for the right word. "DAPPER!"

Marcus drummed his heels on the dining room floor.

"He surely dressed well," Zygolt said.

"Then, who came up with this idea of copying the railroads?" Marcus asked.

"The first Bureau heads had been newspaper editors. Not cops. In that era, most cops could not write or read well enough for Bureau work. These editors understood the value of good public relations."

"So we've got to suck up to the citizens?" Marcus said.

"Why not? We have no police power. No guns or uniforms or politics or anything else that gets in the way. Now, you've distracted your teacher long enough, just to avoid work. Like regular students do. Back to the original question. What do we need from Gretchen who hears full-auto weapons and finds shell casings on her land? Are there any hunters in here?"

"I'd just as lief have animals shoot at me," Marcus said.

"That's Texas talking," I said. "We haven't heard much Texas talk from you yet, Marcus."

"Pour more wine into me. It will come back. Y'all"

Thinking hard formed part of a wine buyer meal. My Showbizzers had to learn how to do it. To give them time to think, I looked at my bandaged knee and wondered if taking the bandage off now would help. As usual, I was wearing cut-off blue jeans.

"Come on, team," I coaxed. "What do we know about shell casings?"

"They are all different!" Koy said. "You taught us that the hammer or the firing pin or whatever the hell, leaves a different impression from gun to gun. So we can tell what gun it came from."

"So what?" Zygolt said.

"Marcus, Koy," I said. "Either one of you know?"

They looked blank. Then they checked each other

"Because the bank robbers fired at the deputies and cops on full auto AK-47s," I said. "It's okay if you don't get this jazz right away. It takes time. I still don't know much. What else?"

"Since the robbers shot at cops, some of the shells will eject onto the ground," Zygolt said. "Your cop buddies have tagged them and scooped them up as evidence. You taught us all this. Probably the robbers wore gloves loading the guns for the holdup. So no prints on the robbery casings. That is logical. My college philosophy professor would sure agree with me. But if you can match them to the casings on Gretchen's land, you check those for prints. Nobody wears gloves loading and practicing BEFORE a robbery. Because there is no reason to.

Nothing ties the practicing group to the robbery group except those casings."

"You scored it, Zygolt," I said. "Keep in mind that it could all be a false trail. The casings might not be the same. Or the prints may be too poor for comparison work. But Crosswaite has a record. His prints are on file. It might work for us."

"So we're doing all this for nothing?" Koy asked.

"Not yet," I said. "We're eliminating possibilities. Now, team, how do we get those shell casings from Gretchen to the cops or, better yet, the FBI?"

"Get on the land and steal them!" Zygolt said. Passion played in her eyes and voice.

"Legally, they're garbage. Garbage has no protection against theft. Anything else?"

"Yeah. You taught us that the courts do not care how the evidence got before. 'The silver platter doctrine.' U.S. vs. Weeks, 1914."

"You Showbizzers make me proud," I said. "Putting your memories into my crackpot idea."

For a minute, we all basked in that feeling, with the wine helping.

The wine was numbing my nerves. My fingers kept working on my knee bandage and unraveling it. Then the bandage lay on the floor. Snowball glared at it and barked.

An angry red scar circled the front of my bare knee.

"Look at that," I said. "That scar will outlive me."

"Give it a month or two out here," Koy said. "And I can wash it in a Chinese ointment for you. Help it clear it up."

Tonight's wine was changing Koy. Maybe she was getting used to me. Or maybe the wine was blurring my own reality.

"Courts do not HAVE to care where evidence comes from," I said. "But they might. A judge can always mistrust how you got evidence and exclude it. So, when you can, get permission from the property owner. How do we do that?"

"Use an honest direct approach," Koy said." Like you say. It's not hard to find somebody named Gretchen in a town this size. One person only. No group approach. Explain who we are and why we care."

"Thirty thousand reasons," Zygolt said. "All of them green."

"Ask her for permission to bring the casings to the cops," I said. "Get a signed release if you can. Try to give them to FBI Agent Merilee Combs at the Basta Resident Agency in the Post Office Building. Any other agent will do. The FBI is much better at not losing evidence. Volunteers for this job?"

Zygolt looked around the room. Her blue eyes showed redness from the wine.

My knee moved. A dull pain flushed through my leg.

"I'll do it," she said. "Marcus, give me the info on Roger's home address. Better yet, his work address. I'll go turn an ankle or faint in front of his job. All men are fools, just like *True Romance* magazine said. He'll give me Gretchen without even knowing it."

"Max, why don't we just give Gretchen's information to the FBI?" Koy asked. "They can go out to her place and get the shells their own damn selves. Don't we pay taxes for that?"

"I'll call Merilee and ask her to do it," I said. "But she won't. It is not a red-hot clue. As you said, many militia groups shoot off pieces around here. These shells could come from them. Unless she is a very unusual agent, she will have to give her time to better and stronger leads. Or other cases."

"To slake my own curiosity," Zygolt asked, "how many other cases would she likely have at one time?"

"In a place like Basta, about twelve to fifteen active open cases," I said. "And she must run down leads from other agents far away, testify in court and write a gazillion reports to keep her bosses happy."

"Would she have to write a report about going to Gretchen's place?"

"At least three reports," I said. "To different parts of her Bureau. And all the reports say the same thing."

"My God in Heaven," Zygolt said. "You're right. She won't go to Gretchen. I wouldn't."

"Neither would I," Koy said. She hiccoughed. "Brain-dead government."

"If I wasn't working in this bank, I would not have gotten this mother-kissing wonderful great, $30,000 tip," Marcus said. "Or the next one. The next one might be even better."

"Give," I said.

Marcus had never seemed this happy to me. He beamed his white smile under the tousled dark hair and burning eyes.

"The bank is not supposed to let me look at current accounts until they clear me on my background and credit check."

"Good luck with that," Koy said. "You're a casino gambler and a ladykiller."

"But I can sneak into closed accounts and root around as much as I want. And there's one for or an Elsa Santee at 89546 Calico Road in the mountains."

I clapped, slowly. The others all joined in after a pause.

It was Show Business, after all.

"Terrific, Marcus," I said. "We are going to check that address and stake it out for when Crosswaite visits his old mama. Who wants to do stakeout duty with me?"

CHAPTER 23

Crosswaite Wants to Destroy Basta

The next morning, I tried to stay flat in bed, still savoring the wine and food from last night. My knee throbbed with pain. It felt unprotected without the bandage on it. The scar still held angry red colors.

A car crunched into the dirt and gravel between our buildings. It was a sheriff's unit with Enrique Mendoza driving. Clytemnestra's red hair flamed in the back seat.

They piled out.

"Morning," Enrique said through the window. He had a haircut now. The hooked nose stood out between the merry blue eyes in the cherub's face. "I'm bringing back one sober-thinking young actress."

Clytemnestra looked happier today than she had before. Her fair skin was lightly tanned now from spending more time outdoors. She wore a light gray shirt and matching pants with the words "San Risa County" stamped in big black letters on both.

"That seems pretty quick for de-tux," I said. "Clytemnestra, can you stay longer there?"

"'course I could."

"That's right," Enrique said. "Coming back today was her idea. She has an open sentence."

"Clytemnestra, how about a couple more days in De-Tox?" I asked. "It'll go by quickly and you'll feel better."

"No way, Jose. I feel better just getting back here. And I miss my family here. And you with your cop teaching lectures."

"You're not an actress for nothing," I said. "And you're learning how to play this scene as you improv on it."

"It's the truth."

"And no more undercover bar crawling, okay?" I said. "We got enough to work on already. Is that a deal?"

"No more bar stuff," she said. "I agree. It's a waste of time anyway."

"And don't go back into Funky Butts bar," Enrique said. "You've been banned, okay? What are you going to tell your drinking buddies about De-Tox?"

"De-Tox sucks," Clytemnestra said. "All the food tastes the same. It's like the Army."

"How would you know?"

"She passed our de-tox course here," Enrique said. "I don't know how."

"Cheating," Clytemnestra said.

"She's fulfilled her alternative sentence. Doesn't owe the damn county anything."

"I never did. That whole arrest mess was a humbug and a roust. Oh, I'm so tired. Hate getting up this fricking early. I'm going to get upstairs, grab a shower and snooze. Join me, Deputy?"

"You already asked me," Enrique said. "I guess that you forgot. I'm on duty. Thanks for not raising more hell than you did raise."

Maybe she was enjoying this morning's role of the wayward actress learning her craft through the mean streets and lockdown.

"Thanks for everything, Enrique," she said, giving him her Cheshire Cat smile. "Is it all right to give you a hug?"

"I can't stop you," he said. "Doubt any man could."

She hugged him, ground her hips into his to remind him and scampered over to the Showbizzer house.

"There's a little gal headed for either a movie career or a big smash-up," he said. "I wish I knew which."

"Me, too. But she's not the only one acting a part around here. Enrique, you being a Basque. How do you switch that Southwestern desert rat accent off and on like you do?"

"Just happens, I suppose. I've got something for you about Crosswaite from our files. Don't tell a swinging damn soul that you got it from me."

"Deal."

He went back into his patrol unit and came out with a clipboard.

A faded photograph was on top of the papers. A round-faced youngster with dark hair and sideburns smiled at the camera. He was wearing the same gray uniform that Clytemnestra had on. He looked like someone coming out of a service station shed to fill up your car with high-test and check the oil with a joke or two. In the photo, his foxy friendly eyes hinted that he knew a lot of them.

"That's Crosswaite?" I said. "He looks like a puppy dog!"

"Wayne Alan Crosswaite. One of the deputies in lockup had taken this for kicks and then left it lying around. Sgt. Caulk has his official folder with the 'hard card' on where he served sentences."

"I can't believe that he looks this friendly."

"He's not. You heard what he did to our badge-heavy kid deputy, right? We don't have enough for a warrant on him for the bank robbery-murder yet. But that's just a matter of time."

"Enrique, there's a woman who heard full-auto shooting on her property before the robbery. Then she found some shell casings on the ground. Could you go out there and see if the shells match the guns used in the robbery-murder?"

Enrique looked like he wanted to scratch somewhere but could not reach the spot.

"Well, the detectives have that case now," he said. "They don't like us fooling with their cases. It could screw up their court trial, too many deputies involved. Have this lady call in and speak to the detectives. They'll be glad to help her."

"Could you go talk to her?"

"It would amount to the same thing. She'd give me the son of a gun shells and I'd be stuck with booking them 'found property-possible evidence.' They would not be happy with me."

"That's what I thought," I said. "Okay. Just wanted to get your feedback on it."

Inside the house, the Showbizzers were greeting Clytemnestra with shouts. It was Homecoming Day. Music from *West Side Story* played from the system. Zygolt was probably reliving her dances in that show.

Coffee brewed and bacon cooked, making me hungry.

Hopefully, they would not smoke a joint and blow the aroma this way while Deputy Mendoza was still here.

"What's the hard card say on him?" I asked.

"Five ten, one eighty-five, brown and blue, no tattoos. Kinda rare in these kids breaking bad now. Usually they're tatted out all over their bodies. Knife scars on both hands. Defensive wounds, they call them. Another knife scar, left ribcage, when he was sixteen. Spent a week in the hospital behind that. Seems like he got into it with a Mexican gang in the Churros de Oro bar."

"Where's this bar?"

"It's not. The owner torched it for insurance fraud. When we were about to bust him for that, he blew himself up."

"Lot of good karma right there," I said. "What did Crosswaite work at?"

"That's the surprise right there. Library assistant. Then researcher out at the Calico Early Man Site along Route 15. Smart kid. That's Bureau of Land Management. They tested dozens of local kids for the job, but he got it."

"Bright kid. What's this place again?"

"They've been digging out there for years and keep finding things. In the 1960s, hunters found funny stones there and brought them to our county museum. An archaeologist expert dated them as manmade tools as far back as 200,000 years old. The oldest site in this hemisphere. The media is always talking about it."

"Really? Surprised I never heard of the place."

"Well, other scientists ran tests and claimed the stones were just natural eroded. But some around here don't believe 'em. Big fuss."

"I just can't see Crosswaite as an archaeologist," I said.

"Just helping them out. But they liked him. Since that is a federal land site set up by the BLM, he was on his way to being a full-time federal employee with Civil Service bennies and a pension. Do you know what that means?"

"It means that you can stop working forever."

"Right. Just ask the Post Office. Except for some of our buddies in the FBI and such-like, it's time to take life easy. But Washington kept cutting funds for archaeology projects and delaying his permanent spot. There was nothing that anybody could do."

"You can't goose Washington into moving faster."

"So, he got kind of bitter about that. Drinking a lot more, fights, smashed up some cars and fled the scene. The Feds dropped him like a bad habit when that happened. No career possible working on the site once you step into that mess there. Arrests for Unlicensed Handgun, Felony Evading, Defaced Firearm in Possession. Those warrants were still outstanding when he met up with that deputy. From then on, we feel like he declared war on San Risa County and all us who live here."

"He likes guns?" I asked.

"According to his rap sheet, what the hell do you think?"

"I don't think that he's into tai chi."

Enrique turned his head towards the car. Maybe he was thinking about how many speeders he could ticket today and keep his Sergeant Caulk happy.

"Enrique, who deals guns around here that's not legit?"

"Oh, no. I'm not sending you and your kids out to buy guns."

"No, you're not," I said. "We don't want them or need them for the way that we will work. I want to know where Crosswaite might go to buy, sell or trade."

Enrique's face closed down again as he thought.

"Enrique, it will take me one phone call to some reporter at *The Desert Dispatch* to get this information," I said. "Every gun dealer, legit or otherwise, gets a violation sometime. It's public record. Or I call a friend at Alcohol, Tobacco and Firearms in New York and have him tell me. All you're doing is making me work a bit harder."

"Behind Santiago's Garage on Williams Street near Pico Street," he said. "There's a mechanic named Jesse got his own place to fix flats. He's gone down a few times for gun violations. Supposed to supply whatever you need, no questions asked."

"Thanks, Enrique."

"Remember, Royster, you didn't get this info from me. Our boss does not like us helping outsiders with official stuff. I don't want to be stuck inside, working the jail forever.

"Crosswaite threatened your town, Enrique," I said.

"There was a snitch I had on narco cases," Mendoza said. "He usually tried to sell me a lot of bull for ten bucks a pop. Said that someone, he couldn't say who, planned to black out Basta and take it apart. Some drunk in the Eagles' Tavern on Main Street was mouthing off."

This was getting better. My hand went to Mendoza's heavy arm.

"Will you let me talk with your snitch?" I asked. "Just two minutes."

"He couldn't tell you much now, Max. He's dead last week. Smoking in bed and he lit himself up. Took out his room."

"Anyone check for arson?"

"Why would they? He never gave much value as a snitch. Nobody liked him. Nobody cared. He was full of hot air."

"Nice epitaph," I said.

"About what he deserved," he said.

We shook hands like cops.

He curled up back into his car and pulled out back onto Main Street.

"Max, a hangover from a high-end wine often helped me making friends on the morning after," Zygolt said from the doorway, a large bag slung over her shoulder.

"Why?"

"Because it strips away your inhibitions and you want to get closer to who you're talking to."

"Zygolt, why are you telling me this?"

"Because I'm off to find Roger and then Gretchen, the lady with shells in her backyard. And when we look in each other's eyes, she will know that she and I want the same thing. Mister Crusty or Crumbum or whatever-"

"Crosswaite," I said.

"We both want the same thing," she said. "Crosswaite out of circulation."

"So Gretchen whosis and I will have some good girl talk about the empty bullets on her property. And I'll get that written consent and the dead bullets from her. You just watch me."

Zygolt was wearing her Showbizzers T-shirt and a pair of tailored bluejeans that showed off her solid dancer's legs. It looked as if she had picked out the ensemble to give a message.

"I'm going out on this stage a nobody and I'm coming back a dancing crime fighter," she said.

Her face held a look that nothing could stop.

Wanting to protect her aura, I shut up and watched as she got into her Jeep roared away.

⇟

Inside the house, Clytemnestra was back in her regular sports clothes and going through breakfast like a redheaded buzz saw. Marcus and Koy were watching a monster movie on their laptop.

"Marcus, I need a volunteer driver," I said. "Take you just a half hour. Drop me, wait nearby, and I'll come to you."

"I'll do it," Koy said. "Snowball needs to see things."

"I'm afraid not, Koy," I said. "Just Marcus."

"Why not me?"

"Yeah, why not?" Marcus asked. "I got a big soft head from last night's drinking and was planning to take a nap."

"I can't ask Koy to drive me," I said. "Asians stand out in Basta. She would be noticed a lot sooner than you would be. And this could be dangerous."

"For who?" Marcus asked.

"Both of us. My leg's still too stiff to drive so I have to ask you."

"Or me," Clytemnestra said. "Danger? I like danger."

"Your red hair," I said.

"Phooey on that. I'll wear my big floppy sun hat. Nobody will see the hair unless they cut off my head. I like the danger. Let's go!"

CHAPTER 24

Calico Early Man Site

"No, Clytemnestra," I said. "There's too much risk in this. Marcus will drive. Nobody pays much mind to two jokers in a car. But you have star power. Everyone wants to be near you."

"Horse feathers and petrified apple butter," she said. "I know some other words, too. But a day without risks bores me silly."

"Can you please copy your notes written in the bars and send them to Zygolt's laptop?" I asked. "That beery gossip that you're getting is good stuff. That's how we'll break the case."

"You like Marcus' stuff better," she said.

"Jealous actress," Marcus said.

"That's because he's in the bank!" Clytemnestra said. "Do you know what I could do if I was that damn bank?"

"Yup," I said. "You could put the gypsy twist on that bank president, gratify him that way and make him jump naked through the front window at high noon."

Marcus drove me along Williams Street. It ran parallel to Main Street, up a slight rise.

"There's Pico over there," I said. "And there's the Flats Fixed shop. I'm scared going in there because the joker Jesse is supposedly dripping in guns."

"Then don't go in."

"That's a really great idea. But I won't act on it. Don't stop here. I don't want this car seen and remembered by him. Drive to Main Street and dump me. Give me a half hour. If I'm not out by then, can you get me out?"

"Got a United Parcel deliveryman's uniform in the trunk," he said. "Left over from my play, *Tenting Tonight*. And the shoes. If you're not out, I'll put on the duds and hammer on his goddamn door. Everybody loves United Parcel bringing them surprises. Believe me, he won't turn me away."

"Then what will you do? He's a gun dealer, for Chrissake."

"I added tear gas pepper spray to the costume. He'll get a face full of it. With his eyes shut, he ain't shooting this child. Then I beat him down and look for you. Simple."

"You're a vicious fella," I said.

"No acting jobs coming in enrage this artist. I fantasize about beating up my agent. It's goddamn easy for me to channel that rage at strangers."

He obeyed my instructions to drop me off and drove away.

❧

Both my legs, the good right and the weak left, shook. I was operating on one crutch now, under my left armpit. It made feel like a gutty Long John Silver, swinging his way through Treasure Island.

The flats shop was as dark as I expected. Rings of tires lay humped on their sides. Tools lay on the floor. Oil puddles gleamed. Something chemical, like a bonding agent, fouled the air. It turned my stomach over. Or maybe I was just afraid.

The mechanic surprised me. He had a long scraggly beard, a ponytail, thick gladiator arms and was sitting in an old-looking tin wheelchair.

"Partner," he said in a Southern drawl, "what can I do you for?"

"You the Man here?"

"That's me. Don't let the contraption throw you. I just got hit with a degenerative muscle disease of some kind. Can't even remember what it is called. Most customers don't know I got it yet. So keep it cool, under your hat. Okay?"

"Won't tell anybody."

He smiled, showing pearly teeth amid the bushy beard. Suntanned and solid, he dwarfed the wheelchair. Some clinic had probably jammed his big frame in it and wheeled him out to get rid of him.

"That'll fit just fine," I said. "Because I'm here on the quiet myself. Looking for something to protect myself."

"Come over here, then," he said, doing a deft turn to a door. "Everything that I got is all legal and clean as a baby's butt."

He opened the door.

It reminded me of the Coney Island penny arcades when I was a kid. Riches were stacked high, to tempt the sucker putting his nickels into the machine and hooking onto a treasure.

But these treasures were all guns. Hunting and military rifles lined the walls. Their stocks, walnut, oak, cherry wood, gleamed. The bolt actions lay open, to avoid rust. Shotguns with hand carved stocks of birds or game fleeing lay at my feet. Someone had burnished their stocks and blued their metal parts with loving care.

Gold-plated Winchester Repeaters with wooden stocks so polished that they looked wet hung on one wall. A silver-plated German Luger formed this banquet's centerpiece. Pocket automatics with pearl handles, looking as cute as cookies, lay in zippered black leather cases.

"I doubt that I've ever seen a room like this," I said.

"True that, big fella. If this disease takes me to the Unanswered-Question-in-the-Sky, I'd like to think that this room got left behind as my memento."

"You should be proud of the work that you put into it."

"Oh, I am," he said. "Be sure of that."

Our Showbizzer cover story felt thin, in front of these all this weaponry.

"I'm looking to pay a debt," I said. "Fella named Crosswaite."

"Sure," he said. The big bearded head nodded. But something in his face changed. Fear spiraled in me. "He's got new digs. Got the address in my office there."

I turned to leave.

He did another deft turn. The chair jumped forward. It hit my one crutch. I fell forward. His hand caught my shirt and yanked it up.

"Only Feds ask about Crosswaite!" he shouted. "And you smell of cop. You can't play-act no way! Lousy Feds! Jackals."

"I'm no Fed."

"Always after Crosswaite," he said. His free hand frisked me. "Where's your wire, Fed? And your piece?"

"Let go!" I tried twisting free.

His hand dropped and punched my gut. By instinct, I hit back. I fell back against the wall. He flopped out of his wheelchair.

Both of us hit the floor, throwing strikes. We hit each others' shoulders, earlobes or the wall behind us.

"Knock it off!" I said in pure New Yorkese. "This is stupid."

"You Feds keep sniffing around me for Crosswaite. Got nothing left to protect! I had a bellyfull of you."

"I'm freelance. Freelancer than you could know. Let's both get up and do some business."

He reared back on the floor.

"Touch me and we start the ball again," he said. "Just leave me alone and get out of my place."

"Buddy, I didn't mean, knock you down," I said. "That's not how I work."

"Just get," he said.

I got.

He stayed on the floor.

"Wonder how long I got?" he said. "With this muscle disease deal, I mean."

***

When I got my crutch going quick from adrenaline, I made it to Main Street. Marcus was waiting in the Jeep. He wore his United Parcel uniform and belt tear gas holder.

"You're early," he said.

"Just drive."

"Do you know that your mouth is bleeding some?"

"See the above comment."

***

Back at what I called home, I took a cold shower that cooled the hot pipes of my body. Transients in places like this used cheap thin soap bars. I used the soap that came with the room. It filmed all over my body. My mouth, my left knee and the wild pig scar sent me messages that they were unhappy.

"Koy," I murmured in the shower. "This tough cop needs to see something clean."

After the shower, I dressed and crutched over and translated my message so that moderns like Koy could understand it.

"Maybe you have the wine hangover, too," she said. "And you think that me driving you will cure you."

"Bring Snowball," I said. "You said before that he needs to get out."

❧

We followed dark brown government road signs onto U.S. 15.

The highway brought us through vast expanses of desert. Land rose and dipped on either side of the road. Service roads stopped. This was the only road cutting into the wilderness. To the south, railroad tracks loped about a quarter of a mile away.

Another road sign read "Calico Early Man Site – Property Managed by the U.S. Bureau of Land Management."

An arrow told us to leave the highway. We did and looped to the north on the only road.

Our road turned to dirt. We bumped along. Ruts made our Roadmaster dance. Snowball objected.

Rocks spanged against our wheels some more.

Koy started objecting. Snowball had used better language.

We came to a wire fence about four feet high. One road forked inside. We followed that, rocking some more.

A wooden shack with three glass windows lay to our left. An electric generator stood next to it.

Pits dug into the earth yawned off the roadway. Workers sifted screens of dirt back and forth.

"The media keeps calling this place California's Unknown-Wonder-of-the-Century," Koy said. "They archeologists dig through the dirt and hunt for man-made tools or other artifacts. It makes me feel spooky. I mean, Ancient Man crawling all around here. I couldn't sleep out here if I tried."

"Archaeology doesn't pull you to it?" I asked.

"Yuck!"

A blocky man in an Army style jungle hat stepped from the shack. His silver glasses glinted under pure white hair. Sun had reddened his smiling face.

To our right, a group watched another man hurl a wooden spear into a twenty-foot sand pile. The spear stuck in a wooden board in the pile.

"This your first time here, folks?" he asked us. "This is the oldest place in the Western Hemisphere. Scientists here found flint tools that went back 200,000 years."

The man holding the wooden spear approached. A white beard livened his face under the hat. He was laughing like a boy and had a leather strap wrapped around his right forearm.

"You just missed my atl-atl demonstration," he said, speaking rapidly. He had the precise speech of a professor, without the local drawl.

"What's an 'atl-atl'?" Koy asked.

"This device on my arm here," he said. "It gives force to my throwing this wooden spear. Primitive Man here at Calico had to hunt animals much bigger than he was. To survive, the man had to hunt with a group. The group would find the animal and try to surround it. If they got too close, the beast would kill some of them."

"What were they hunting with?" Koy asked.

"Hand-axes and knives made of stone, rocks in slings like David and Goliath and pointed wooden spears like this one. But the spears would only pierce the animal's hide up close. So they invented this atl-atl here. You strap it on your forearm and wrist like a big leather bandage."

He showed us.

"Fit the butt of the spear into the slot on your wrist. Lock it in with your fingers."

The spear's end sat in the leather slot between his fingers.

"Then, you aim and fling your spear."

His arm flew forward. The spear went through the air. It hit the wooden board in the sand-pile and stuck there.

"Wow," I said.

"These spears would mostly wound the animal," he went on. "Then the bravest hunter in the group would approach the critter with a stone knife. Like the animal, we have our femoral artery and groin exposed to anyone beneath us. If we can't see them, we can't defend ourselves. So the Mr. Pleistocene would try to roll underneath it. Once he was under the vulnerable soft parts, he would rip upwards with that knife and hope to gut the animal.

"Meanwhile, spears from other atl-atls would strike and distract the beast while the knifer was trying to hit an artery. Here you go, Red. Take a try."

"I got to put the crutch down," I said. "I haven't tried standing without it."

"This is a gol-dang magical place," the man with the glasses in the jungle hat said. He exhaled a laugh through his smiling mouth. "It's a damn good place to heal."

The crutch went down. I balanced and picked up the atl-atl and strapped it to my arm. Then I put another thin wooden spear in place with my left.

"They didn't have iron yet," the man said. "So these old boys would sharpen the wooden point or wedge a sharp piece of flint onto the tip. They'd tie it on with animal gut or leather. It was just a short range weapon. The atl-atl made it safer at longer distances."

I flung it. The spear lanced forward. It flew straight and true and stuck in the wood.

"You're good," he said. "Not many get the right timing on when to release the spear. Fewer get it to stick the first time."

"Will it help my resume?" I asked.

"Never can tell, hoss. I'm Chris Tiesen. Manage this place for BLM."

We needed to break the ice more.

"Koy, let me teach you to toss it," I said.

Koy did well throwing the atl-atl. The men clustered near her and talked.

Koy gave our names and the cover story about owing Crosswaite cash for dog training. That cover story sounded weaker all the time. But it had to stay the same.

Chris's amiable face knotted as he thought about Crosswaite.

"You sure that it was Wayne?" he asked. "Bright guy about thirty-years old, sideburns, thick hair."

Koy did not flinch. She was recalling our training classes and kept eye contact with the mark.

"I never knew Wayne to have any children," the white-bearded man said, overhearing us. "He used to work here, when he was in high school. One of the quickest minds that I ever saw."

"But the light ladies favor him, Ted," Chris said. "Like as not, he found some grass widow with a couple of kids who wanted to play with their dog."

We stayed still. The rules said to let the mark, the pigeon, in your hustle come to his own conclusion. The operator should only start the idea.

"Haven't seen Wayne since Memorial Day," the white-bearded man said. "By the way, I'm Ted Duninger, the director and curator here. He comes here to relax once in a while. What happened to your leg there?"

"Accumulated *anno domine*. Old age."

"At the museum here, we sell handmade walking sticks. Easier on your body than that crutch. They are way thicker than canes. Plus the proceeds help our research."

Undercover rules said to buy whatever you could to cement a friendship.

I bought a stout walking stick with a leather thong attached, I hefted it like any other weapon. It would do just fine. And no deputy could arrest me for carrying it. It looked innocent and touristy.

Trying to sell our cover story to these archaeologists felt silly.

We left after touring the pits and seeing the ancient tools and weapons dug up there.

"They got no idea where Crosswaite is now," Koy said.

"If they do, they're not telling us," I said. "But that's okay. He'll be back there again. And so will we."

Chapter 25

Stagecraft

"Why are we going back now?" I asked Koy. "I want to check that address on Calico Road for Crostwaite's mama."

"Snowball has to be fed," Koy said. "I should have done it sooner. That's why I worry about money so much. He eats more than I do and weighs more than I do."

"I see where that could be a burden."

"Then I'll go with you to watch that woman's trailer."

"You will? You're full of surprises, Koy. Slow down here before coming into our place. I want to check things out first."

"Do you think that someone could be watching us?"

"Why not? That cardboard sheriff or even Merilee's FBI buddies. Once you try helping cops for free, they suspect you of everything. I also worry that Crosswaite or some other subject could be scoping us out."

"That scares me."

"Me, too. That's why I'm being careful today. Californians love their cars so much that anyone watching will be in a car. That makes them comfortable. And vulnerable." We pulled back into the Route 66 Arms, with me cranking my neck around.

"There's Chick's Chevy," I said. "Who has that green Pinto?"

"Maybe someone is visiting."

We got out. Snowball bounded onto the ground. Koy trained him to obey simple commands like "Sit" or "Heel."

Snowball did not respond well to the idea of training on an empty stomach.

"When do we work our way up to a command like 'Attack?'" I asked.

"Poor little baby is hungry," she said, hugging him with her arms around his wooly head. "Maybe he'll do better after lunch."

"Maybe he'll do better after Christmas dinner," I said. "Three years from now. That's a goof-off and a chow-hound that you got there."

"My little baby."

Clytemnestra came bounding down the porch steps.

"Max, I got you a new car for your stakeout," she said.

"That Pinto?"

"Yessir. You trained us that you should always switch cars during a stakeout. So I borrowed one from a friend."

"Again, I don't want to come off like the heavy father, but what kind of friend? Who loans a car out anymore with insurance and all the other headaches involved? Damages? Tickets?"

"Dutch Door," she said. "He's a shade-tree mechanic. Got lots of cars. I know him from the Eagles bar."

"Sounds lovely. Why does he loan you a car?"

"Oh. Because he wants to be my Sugar Daddy. He told me so."

"How romantic," I said. "How old is he?"

"Pretty far. He's about your age."

"Thank you."

The ancient Pinto would never stand out. Most owners would deny having one. I scanned it, got inside and tested the horn, ignition and gas. Bending my bad leg was tough. But I needed to keep doing it.

"Everything seems to work," I said. "In a clunky kind of way."

"Aren't you happy with me?" she asked. "Nobody can trace this car to us."

She hugged me to prove it. I could imagine that Dutch Door was thinking about her often.

"Nobody except Dutch Door," I said. "Yes, Cly. That's good thinking on your part. I'll get it back to you tomorrow."

While Koy fed Snowball, I loaded up our new gift with water bottles, beef jerky, crackers and maps. Two cellphone chargers went in the glove box. After thinking it over, I unloaded my shotgun and put it in the trunk.

"Why are you unloading it?" Koy asked.

"California law. If the shells are touching or near the gun, it is deemed to be loaded. You cannot carry it loaded in the trunk without a hunting license. We'll keep the ten shells in my pockets in case we have to move somewhere with vigor."

"That's silly."

"Let me drive," I said. "I need the practice. It is time that I was a real Californian."

The Pinto's gears clashed but we got on the road anyway, with Snowball snoozing in the back seat.

"Nothing high-tech goes into the desert or the Calico Mountains," I said. "No GPS or anything like that. Fort Irwin Army Base goes on for about sixty miles into the desert. So does Fort Drum for the Marines. All that is off limits to us civilians. That makes it tougher for us. We just have to run along Calico Road until we find a trailer or a house near where those numbers would be."

"Would the bank give an account to someone in a trailer?" Koy asked.

"They have to. Unless they want a lawsuit. You can live under a table at In-'n-Out Burgers and still demand your right to bank your money."

❧

Driving this car after my injury with Koy alongside felt as strange as cantering a horse around the Rings of Saturn. My fingers gripped the wheel, hoping that the strangeness would melt soon.

"It's been a long time since I staked out anywhere as a cop," I said. "Even then, I wasn't real good at it."

"No?"

"As a matter of truth, I was no worldshaker of a cop. Tried to get through each shift without harming an innocent.

A million rules contradicted each other in our Patrol Manual. Nobody who was rich and white cared much. Unless it annoyed them."

"It's not a world that I ever cared about."

"Who do you think stops dopers from stealing Snowball for today's crack money?"

She shivered and reached an arm back to pet Snowball.

"I see how you give of yourself to teach and protect us Showbizzers, as you call us," she said. "Seems like something powerful in you. And I keep wondering why you do it."

"Maybe because policing is too important to be left to the deputies," I said.

We kept driving.

Late afternoon sun lit the Calico Mountains.

"We should be on Calico Road now," I said. "By the process of elimination. There is no other road."

"But there are no houses out here."

"Some dirt roads. They could go sixty feet and stop at a fence. Or they could go the hundred-and-forty-three miles to Las Vegas. Nobody can tell."

We crested another rise.

"We need to stay quiet tonight, if we ever find this place," I said. "Can Snowball hold his mud?"

"Excuse me?"

"Can he stay quiet?"

"Of course. How much barking do you hear from your room?"

Joshua trees sprouted to the south.

Winds picked up and shook the Pinto.

"There's a sand devil," she said, pointing. "Like a miniature cyclone. Winds swirl the dust way up in the sky. Got them in your Manhattan?"

"Not yet. Koy, we don't have any of this stuff in my Manhattan. How did you get started with training animals?"

"Loved going to the zoo. Other kids, they fool around with each other near the Coke machine. But I'd watch them. Fascinate me. Volunteered after school to clean up the cages of craparoo and feed them and learn their names. Knew so much and held so much wisdom in their eyes. Each had their own personality. More than I could say for my high school chums."

"Did you study them formally?"

"B.S. and an M.A. from Pierce College in L.A. in Animal Studies. The school offered internships in Hollywood, learning to train animals for the movies. The trainers taught me a lot and introduced me around the sets. Films were making us job offers and I loved my work in film."

"Does Snowball have screen credits?"

"Not yet. But he's going to. I supported myself enough to get my parents off my back about finding a husband."

"And you're between movie jobs now?"

"You know better than that. Can't work or enjoy anything or anyone else until I find out about this cancer thing that might be inside me right now." Her voice quavered. "Eating away at my insides whether I'm walking, playing with Snowball, eating, sleeping or showering –"

"Cool it, Koy. You're just working yourself up into a state."

"Don't you care?"

"I care enough to protect you from making yourself sick with worry. Koy, I bet you that a year from now, you'll be a little bored."

"Why, for God's sake?"

"Because you escaped this cancer scare. You'll look back on this month and wonder why you were so worried. Next year, you'll have new fears. You know what we call that?"

"No, what?"

"Progress."

The land darkened. Shadows grew. Then full dark came down.

"We just passed a sign reading 87000," Koy said. "But it does not say what road we are on."

"That's kind of important," I said. "I see some trailers over there against the mountain. Would hate to be the mailman here."

"These desert rats drive into Basta to pick up their mail once a month."

"There's a trailer by itself," I said. "Silver with red trim windows. Trash cans out front. See if you can spot a number."

She squinted.

We passed the trailer.

"Nothing, Max."

"This would frustrate a lesser man."

I pulled a U-turn, stopped and killed the lights.

"What are you doing?" she asked.

"Changing philosophy. It is called method acting by Stanislavsky. We have to stop thinking and feeling like crime fighters. We have to think and feel like something else."

"What?"

"Lovers."

Taking a deep breath, I took my hand off the steering wheel and held hers. She started to pull her hand away.

"Don't do that, please," I said. "After all, we have Snowball here as a chaperone."

"I think he's asleep."

"With one eye open, protecting his mistress. So you do not have to fret about my animal appetites."

We stayed like that, by the roadside.

"Do you still feel like a detective?" I asked.

"That's some kind of trick question. No matter what I answer, I'm in trouble."

"That's okay, Koy. Right now, I don't feel like a cop. I feel like a lover. And I'm the one stepping out on stage now."

Switching the headlights on, I moved the car closer to the trailer. Then I got out and went to my back tire and kicked it like a man checking for a flat. I could always bring it to Old Jesse, the bearded gun dealer.

The trashcans glinted. My eyes scanned them.

As soon as possible, I was back inside the Pinto and driving it away.

⁊

"Bingo!" I said. "That's the trailer that we want. 89546 Calico Road."

"How do you know?"

"Trashcans. Trailer folks don't like putting their numbers or names on trailers. They like privacy. Don't want process servers or cops or insurance snoops finding them. But they don't want others stealing their trashcans. If they do steal them, there will be arguments over who owns the trashcans. So they put the address on them. 89546 Calico Road."

"But we don't know if that's still Crosswaite's mother living there."

"True."

"We don't know if she's hiding him out as a murderer."

"Do you want me to ask?"

At a football field down the road, I pulled off onto the shoulder and killed the lights.

"The nights are the worst times," she said. "When the fears cover me up like killer roots poking into my eyes and throat and making me gag. That's why I try to sleep early."

"Not just tonight but other nights, when you get scared, come talk to me."

A blue Jeep passed us by.

"You loaned me that money," she said.

"General all-purpose loan."

"Do you have that kind of money?"

"I'm afraid to look."

"That's immature talk coming from you," she said. "As an adult, you have certain responsibilities-"

I kissed her.

She pulled away. Her scent mixed with fresh cotton and shampoo. Her head tilted on the seat and the coconut-colored eyes searched my face.

Risking again, I leaned forward and kissed her again.

She stopped. Then she kissed me back.

The Pinto swirled around inside my own head.

"I said so many mean things to you," she breathed. "And you still like me. Are you a masochist?"

"No. I'm a Sagittarius."

"Most men would hate me for giving them such a hard time."

The same Jeep passed by. I could not see the driver.

"Do you let women push you around too much?" she asked.

"I could never find the dividing line."

"Which dividing line?"

"The one that tells me what to do," I said. "When things hurt me, should I leave? Or should I take it as part of life and keep on trying to love?"

"I don't understand that."

"Me neither," I said. "Are you planning more painful remarks?"

She did not answer. I kissed her again. A happy flush warmed my body down past the weak knee and into the New York winter sneakers.

The same Jeep passed us.

I waited until the Jeep's tail-lights had faded.

"Out of the car," I said. The shotgun shells were already in my hands. "Get Snowball out. Don't slam the doors. Just click them shut. Stay low and keep this car at your back and walk forward."

"Why?"

"I'll explain soon. Just do it now."

Chapter 26

Like Hot Dogs

I grabbed the duffle bag, zipped it up and shouldered it. Headlights showed up ahead.

"Don't stop now!" I said. "Keep Snowball quiet."

Thrashing into the desert brush, my bad knee hit something solid. Pain skyrocketed through me. My stick dropped.

Headlights washed over me.

A car engine buzz sawed.

I dropped.

Thirty feet behind me, the Pinto exploded. The light showed Koy's stricken face framed by black hair. Snowball barked.

The same headlights swept across the desert scrub. Maybe he had heard Snowball. But he might think that it was a stray dog.

The headlights swung one way and then another. The driver was using his lights to search the area.

Flames flowered behind me.

My shaking hands fed a shell into the shotgun breech by feel. Closing it might make too much noise. Racking a shotgun was a sound that every gunman knew. When the flames hit our gas tank, enough noise would cover my shotgun noise.

The gas tank blew.

A huge CRUMP! noise sounded.

The shotgun racked the round.

Koy came back to me. Snowball followed.

"Shoot him!" she said.

"Hush!"

"What's the damn gun for?"

"Quiet. Go flat. Keep that dog of yours quiet."

The headlights shifted away from us. The engine got louder. I froze. He might be looking over the landscape, trying to find us.

The headlights left us.

My fingers pushed four more shells into the shotgun. I did not have to rack it again. The spring action fed the shells.

The headlights went down the road.

"Why didn't you shoot?" she hissed.

"That's for later. Are you okay? Can you walk? How is Snowball?"

"Of course we can walk. I'm too scared to stay here."

"I'll go first. You follow."

"Why?" she asked. "Goddamn it, Max."

"Pretend that we're in Myanmar."

"Huh?"

"Burmese men make their wives and concubines walk behind them."

Our Pinto lay where we had been kissing. The horrid smell of burning gas and rubber choked me. Cold winds blew.

"Scratch one Pinto," I said.

"Was that Crosswaite?"

"Wasn't a meteorite."

"Why would he burn a car just sitting on the road like that?"

"When we find him, I'll be sure to ask him."

"I'm already cold."

"You've been out here longer than I have. So you know that the Mojave is cold at night, even in summer. We'll stay on the road. When we see headlights, we jump off and hide. We can't chance them coming back in another car."

"This is bringing out the bossy part of you," she said.

"When it comes to staying alive, I'm a downright dictator. Maybe you forget that whoever that was wanted us to cook and pop like hot dogs in our skin. Pardon me, Snowball.

Maybe he could see the Pinto was empty. He might be an over-achiever type who likes to leave no witnesses and is coming back with an army of cutthroats. Let's walk."

We trudged. My walking stick helped some but my knee worked slowly. Back in Manhattan, the idea was to build my knee back to full strength by slow degrees. Tonight was not helping.

Far across the desert, from time to time, we saw some headlights moving.

Then some lights roved along our road. The three of us went off the road and knelt down. The shotgun came out of the long green duffle bag. My right index finger stayed near the safety. The barrel pointed near the unknown headlights.

The barrel wobbled from my nerves. Getting firebombed seemed like the ugliest way to die.

The headlights went away.

"Why didn't you shoot when they bombed our car?" she asked. "Are you some kind of wimp? Afraid to pull the trigger?"

"You civilians always think that we cops can shoot whenever we want," I said. "So you want us to send bullets flying for anything."

"Perhaps —"

"You can't say 'perhaps' when you're running for your life across the desert at night with Snowball."

"I'll say what I please."

"Apparently. Cops only shoot to defend themselves or an innocent victim. Same with civilians. The law says that if I shoot and kill someone for burning my empty car, then I'm guilty of murder. And I'm a civvy right now, remember?"

"But he might still find us and kill us."

"And if I had shot at him back there, without a clear target, what would I hit?" I asked. "Maybe nothing. And he would know we were alive and armed. If he had buddies with him, they could fan out and hunt us down at their leisure. Our best chance for surviving is them thinking that we are cooked in that Pinto already."

The desert winds grew colder. We found a grove of stunted trees and lay down to rest.

Koy came to rest on my arm. We lay like that, cuddling to stay warm. I kissed her and she kissed me. Her scent filled me.

Snowball-the-Attack-Wonder-Dog rested at our feet. The oddest trio in California lay down to sleep under the bright sky shot through with stars.

"You still didn't pay me for the gas," she murmured.

❧

Dreams of the white-heat firebomb chased me through sleep. In the dream, for some reason, I wore a tan trenchcoat with short pants. My scarred left knee sprouted pink scar tissue all around it.

My beard had grown back in the dream. A large tuft of my red beard, trimmed with white hair to show my age, stuck out.

More cars behind me burst onto flames in the dream. Snowball ran alongside me, barking. Men with sharpened hand-knives, like ancients might have worn at Calico Early Man Site, ran after me. Someone flung a wooden spear from an atl-atl at me.

I woke up sweating in the cold wind. The dream faded from my mind.

Koy lay asleep on my left arm, cramping it. Snowball lay next to her.

"Easy, Max," I whispered aloud. "The dream is over."

Just to make sure, I untangled myself from Koy and got my walking stick. Getting the end of the stick dug into the ground, I stood up. My knee joints crackled.

Nothing moved in the desert landscape. We were sleeping about thirty feet from the road. No headlights would catch us if they came down it.

Looking around again and checking my shotgun in the duffle bag, I tried scrunching my body back to sleep. Cold still clawed at me. I tried burrowing down deeper between Koy and Snowball's bodies.

Gray morning finally came.

We got up and watched the road.

By my guessing, we had walked about three miles from the burnt-out Pinto by now. I hoped that it was far enough. The fire bomber might come looking for us still.

Engine noise cut the air.

Making sure that we could run back into the brush, I came onto the road with Koy and Snowball behind me. The duffle bag hung from my shoulder by the strap. The shotgun lay inside, with the barrel pointed down, ready to draw and fire.

A ranch truck bounced into view. My pulse hammered my throat. Just as we had switched cars, maybe the fire bomber had done the same thing.

A white straw cowboy hat bobbed above the steering wheel. He slowed when he saw Koy and Snowball. He was a Latino worker about forty and the truck looked like he was using it every day and did not have enough quality free time for randomly firebombing old Pintos.

Waving both arms, Koy whistled at him. I leaned on my stick and slipped my right arm into the duffle bag.

He stopped and leaned out of the window.

"What happened?" he asked.

"Car trouble," I said. This morning, I was a minimalist. There was no loose talk.

"Yeah, man?" he asked.

"It overheated," I said. "Can you get us to where there's some cellphone coverage?"

He said he would. The three of us refused to share the front seat with him. After last night, I was cutting back on chances. We stepped into the truck's bay. It smelled of disinfectant that was fighting the manure stink. The manure was winning.

The duffle bag stayed open all the time, my hands next to it.

He brought us to a gas station at a crossroads. The gas pump jockey called 911 for me and put me on the phone with Sheriff's Department.

In the tiny bathroom, I unloaded the shotgun and crammed the shells into Koy's shoulder purse.

She would hold the shells in her bag.

As long as I held the duffle bag and shotgun, California law called the shotgun unloaded because another person had the shells. My research had me scratching my head.

Three deputy cars rolled to the station. A lumpy Sheriff's Detective named Avery, in a seersucker jacket and Army pants got, out of one and asked me some questions.

"What in the blue blazes were you doing out here in nowhere?" he began. "I mean, gol-dang. No wonder you got trouble."

His questions told me that he wanted to go home right now. Then he ordered a young deputy to take the report and not screw it up.

They acted like I had firebombed my own car.

Then two unmarked cars pulled up. The Sheriff boosted himself out of the second one. Sgts. Gwynn and Caulk, in tan dress uniforms, emerged from the first car. Sgt. Gwynn glared at me and spat on the ground.

The Sheriff strode over to me. His handsome face flamed. It was a great TV camera shot.

"I knew this was going to happen," he said. "You think that you can out-police professionals who spend years in training?"

"That depends on what they did after the training," I said.

"What's in that duffle you got there?"

"Shotgun," I said.

"What?" he shouted. "You're holding a goddamn shotgun near me?"

His deputies heeded his voice.

"It's unloaded, sir," I said. "Empty breech and magazine. No shells anywhere on me. So, pull in your neck."

"Just by chance, I was driving up to Fort Irwin for a luncheon and then your nonsense call comes over the air," he said. "You brought this on yourself. We don't have firebombings here. What were you doing up on that road anyway?"

"Just parked and talking," I lied.

"What's keeping you in this county, Mr. Royster? Would you be interested in another place to try out your crackpot ideas?"

The deputies and Sheriff's Detective Avery shied away from our talk. Maybe they sensed that the Sheriff did not want witnesses.

"Do you usually blame the victim, Sheriff?" I asked. "Someone tries to roast me alive in your county, and it's my fault. Just remember that when you're pointing a finger at someone, three of your own fingers are pointing back at you. My Showbizzers hear chatter that Crosswaite plans to attack and destroy Basta. Like Lidice. Or New Orleans under Murrell. Take this warning, Sheriff."

"All your running around, giving away things and hounding people got you this bombing," he said.

That stopped me. Koy looked over at me, her lips parted.

"You've been watching us?" I asked. "That's how you know about us giving things away. Instead of watching for crimes in your turf, you surveill the people like us who are trying to make Basta safer. Why don't you watch your own deputies goof off, kill time, manhandle innocents and ignore requests for help? It's right out in the open. Just ask any local. If you got the guts."

The Sheriff's hands opened and closed. He looked around but nobody could hear us.

"That's enough stupid talk out of you," he said. "I can jail you on any charge that I want to. Impersonating an officer, filing a false police report, public drunkenness. Then you're in my jail. With killers watching you sleep and thinking about rape. Jail is dangerous. Lawyers can't get you out. Paperwork gets lost. Get you and your fools out of my county. Right now. Or else you may die in my jail."

CHAPTER 27

Trekking

The next morning, I got up while it was still dark and Koy and Snowball were waiting by the Roadmaster.

"I'm scared of these medical tests, Max," she said. "And there's nothing that I can do."

"Oh, yes, there is," I said, opening the back door for Snowball to jump in. "You can smile. When life hits us with these worries, the only thing that we can control is how we react to it. Nothing else."

"Today, I can't smile."

"Then, sing. Join in with me."

We swung the car onto Main Street. I took a deep breath and sang:

> O once upon a time in Arkansas,
> An old man sat by his little cabin door.

"Please, don't sing," she said. "Not today."

My breath sucked in. The audience was canceling the show.

"Okay," I said. "Whatever you wish."

We kept driving.

Koy cried a bit on the drive. Then she slept.

Victorville was waking when we got there.

The clinic had scheduled the tests early because the doctor had a very full day. Phooey on his very full day, I thought.

Waiting for Koy in the big sterile room with the TV blasting out news and weather every half hour, I tried dozing. The media would not let me.

Other patients dragged themselves in and out.

The available magazines were a disaster. It was time to find some books in Basta. In my bag, I had two books.

The first was Thomas Mann's Doctor Faustus, in English, but I did not understand it all.

The other was a poetry anthology from Chaucer to Robert Creeley. Some of that I understood.

My other books were still in my butter-colored room. Once again, I had not planned my day.

After much too long, Koy emerged from the room accompanied by a Latina nurse with dyed blonde hair and rhinestone sharp eyeglasses who was helping Koy walk.

"Rest as much as you need today," the nurse said with a Spanish accent. "Tomorrow, walk a bit. These drugs for the pain will scramble you up a bit. No driving today or tomorrow. After that, you can do what you like."

"Sleep," Koy said.

I took over from the nurse and brought Koy back to the car.

☙

Driving back to the Showbizzer home, I kept sneaking glances at her. She looked beautiful to me. I avoided all the bumps and potholes that I could.

At home, Clytemnestra and Zygolt took her from the car and helped her upstairs. Nobody mentioned feeding or rewarding me so I caned back to my room. Sleep would be a big help.

As soon as I stretched out, my cellphone buzzed.

"Okay," I said into the phone. "I'll get a job tomorrow. I promise."

"This is Special Agent Merilee Combs, FBI," she said. "Is that how you answer the phone?"

"Apparently. It's good to be a civilian, Merilee."

"I hear you. That woman Ms. Zygolt brought us some shell casings from an AK-47 and said that we should contact you with the results."

"Yeah!" I sat upright in bed. "Sure. Or contact any of us. We're a team."

"A team of whatever I don't know," she said. "Because the shells do not match. That gun was not used in the robbery. No markings identical on the firing pin."

My body sank down back on the bed. Maybe Snowball could replace me.

"That gun might belong to the getaway car driver," I said. "He never fired. Or they could have switched guns."

"Whatever, dude. There's no way that I can send the shells in for fingerprinting. So no warrant for Crosswaite. Or anyone. Those subjects are still what we call 'Unsub.' No known subjects."

"Everything points to Crosswaite," I said. "And why is he in hiding?"

"Hiding is not a federal violation. If you'll excuse, I have a pile of paperwork on my desk."

After that, sleep was a relief. I pillowed my left leg to ease the pain and slumbered.

❧

After dark, someone knocked on my door.

"Who?" I shouted like a debonair traveler. "Bill collector, religious pamphleteer or Department Of General Miseries?"

"Marcus, man," his voice came from the other side. "Must be a romantic night. Koy is asking if you could visit her now. She's still groggy. She's got the green door on the second floor. Don't take advantage, Max."

A grin stretched my unshaven whiskers. I could feel the bristles against my lower lip.

"As always, Snowball plays chaperone," I said. "Tell Koy that I'll be right there."

The shower water felt as good as the shaving cream and the cologne against my skin. I selected my best pressed blue jeans.

❧

The other Showbizzers were in their rooms. It was just past seven at night.

My Calico walking stick helped me up the stairs. The green door was off to the right and I tapped on it.

"Come in, Max," Koy said.

Her bedroom was pink and feminine and looked like a high school girl lived here. A blue pennant reading "Maple High Soccer Gals" was thumbtacked to the wall. A soft-looking chair sat next in between two windows. Navajo blankets lumped up the bed.

Koy was under the covers, wearing dark blue pajamas.

"Can you lie down next to me?" she said. "Just that, please. No funny stuff."

"Wouldn't know how to do any funny stuff," I said. "It's been too long."

Lying down next to her exhilarated me. I put the Calico stick under the bed in case I weakened too much to get up again.

"Thanks for driving me," she said. "I'll pay you back for the gas."

"I still owe you gas money," I whispered. "Remember?"

"I hate borrowing money," she said. "Keeps me up nights."

"Sometimes, it's got to be done."

"Hope not," she said. "Don't want to lead you on. Or act like a golddigger with you."

Her voice trailed off. Whenever anything gave her the blues, her accent came back and my ears lost her. It was as if she were diving into a deep pool of Chinese secrets. As an older white man, I could not follow her.

"I don't have much gold to dig."

"But you loaned me. And you didn't know me."

"Firebombing brings us closer together," I said.

"So I called my sister today. Lives in Tyler, Texas, and knows just about everybody there. She got me a job in an animal shelter there."

I rose up on an elbow and looked at her face.

"I'll be staying with her rent-free," she said. "I know that this feels very sudden, this activity. But I'm not that young anymore, to follow my heart and go where it leads me. Time for a mature plan. Working steady, I can send you back the money pretty soon. Faster than if I stay here, washing dogs."

"Ugh," I said.

"I needed to tell you right away. I didn't tell the others yet. Please don't tell them."

"I don't have the energy," I said. It was true. It felt like someone had blackjacked me.

"I'm sorry, Max. Now that I've told you, I feel bad. But relieved, too."

"Yes, indeedy," I said. It felt no good trying to control how I was reacting to this worry. The line of pap that I had fed Koy this morning just did not work for me now. Another false creed crumbled.

"And I want to be alone now," she said.

"I know just how you feel," I said, getting up with my walking stick and left her bedroom with nothing more to say.

CHAPTER 28

Confessing

A day of pain passed.

The weather matched the day with oily gray clouds blocking the sun. Winter reminders crisped the air.

Drafts came into my room for the first time. Southern Californians seldom learned how to insulate their homes. They relied on space heaters, blankets, whiskey or a break in the weather.

Dinner with the Showbizzers would feel heavy tonight. So I dozed in bed until after ten and saved my cash for tonight.

My cellphone buzzed.

I rolled over, groggy and feisty.

"Somebody better be dead," I said into the phone. "Because I was asleep."

"Max, get over to 1648 Elk Street."

"This sounds like Marcus," I said. "What's up?"

"Can't talk. I need backup!"

The call stopped.

Some words triggered me. "Backup" was one of them. Some nights, a cop would be fighting three perps at once and just manage to put that word "backup" over the radio. Then every cop moved. They ran up and down filthy staircases, ran from dinner tables and threw their coffee cups out the radio car windows.

Throwing on clothes, I threw on my sneakers and then made it over to the house. The duffle bag with the shotgun inside it swung from my shoulder.

"Marcus called," I said. "Give me the Roadmaster keys."

"Why?" Koy was in her bathrobe in the kitchen.

"I don't know. Where's Clytemnestra? Could she be in trouble?"

"Why not?" Zygolt said.

"Come with me?" I asked, getting the keys. "Marcus said he needs backup."

"He's just out getting drunk again with his bank buddies. I'm in for the night."

I said something brutal, saw her face harden and I moved for the Roadmaster.

The engine caught and I roared it out of the driveway onto Main Street.

Then the headlights came on.

"Go, man, go!" I chanted.

The speed fever from Patrol washed over me again.

❧

Elk Street was just a few blocks away. I tore down one block, came through an alley down another, looking for 1648.

"Lousy houses in California don't number their houses just like Brooklynites," I said.

Then I saw the Jeep that Marcus drove. I braked, buried my car at the curb and was out moving through the shadows towards the Jeep. The duffle bag stayed in my car.

1648 was a wide flat house painted light blue in darker trim. Wood smoke smell came from the house. Listening hard around the side, I could hear two men inside talking fast. One of them sounded like Marcus.

Words kept coming. But nobody was shouting. Maybe Zygolt was right. Maybe Marcus was exaggerating like drunks did.

"Daddy ain't going to walk up on the porch, stand in front of the door and knock," I said. "That's how cops get killed."

Instead, I stayed off the porch, walked to the front edge of the house and banged on the wall. It was another trick from Patrol. If a perp was waiting inside to shoot you, he would not know where the knock came from.

They hushed.

I knocked again.

Nobody came to the front door. Something was wrong.

My fist hitting the wood was only about twelve feet from the door.

Marcus opened the front door from inside the house.

"Max?" he asked.

With just that word, he sounded drunk.

"Right here," I whispered.

He staggered around and went back inside the door. He bounced against the frame.

"Hold it!" I hissed.

He was already gone.

Cursing, I had to get up on the porch and follow him through the doorway.

I stepped into a living room just inside the door. Marcus and another man swayed in the living room, both holding drinks in their hands.

The fireplace had a good blaze going against the chill night.

The other man had mushroom-colored hair with a hairline that was too low. It made him look hunched over. He should tell his barber. A moustache busied up his face. Tinted eyeglasses rode on a button nose. Muscles showed in his thick arms and neck. He was not tall but thickset and would be hard to move around.

His eyes skipped around the room until they focused on me.

"Who you, dude?" he asked. He was falling down drunk.

"Dan, I told you," Marcus said. "That's Max. He can help you. He's got clout. And big friends with more clout. Tell him your story."

"What good?" Dan asked, waving his drink.

"You'll see. Tell him."

"This son of a gun and I work together at Gila Bank," Dan said. His drink smelled like rum on the rocks. Not much ice floated in it. "Place got held up, blew up frickin' Michelle, can you figure that crap?"

Nodding like a therapist, I waited for more.

"Place gets robbed, right?" he said. "I'm there, scared out of my socks. Not touching any holdup button, no, thank you, sir. Michelle did. Gila Bank thanks you.

"Shots fired, everyone goes haywire. Not just me. Nobody reacts normal. Am I right? Even the bad guys, killers. They shoot Michelle, start cussing a blue streak. One drops a cigarette pack on the floor. Then they're gone. I am in shock. Look at Michelle, you know that the ship has sailed. She's dead sure thing. I toss the cigarette pack into my drawer, I don't know why. Automatic pilot, maybe. I keep seeing Michelle dead there, all blowed up."

"Dan, you're right," I said. "It's not a normal day. Everything went cuckoo."

"Bet your butt," he said. He drank some more.

"Dan, it's not a big deal," I said.

"They could fire me. Not giving them the pack and all. Maybe arrest me. I worry. I can't eat. Can't sleep. It sucks."

I breathed in and out slowly.

"Dan, you are borrowing trouble, my friend," I said. "You had a shock and then you came back to us. That's all."

"My job!" he said. "My job's most important thing in my life right now. They fire me, that's it. In this economy, good-bye, Charlie."

"It won't happen, Dan," I said. This was going to test all my street con skills.

"That's what the actor there Marc said. You boys are optimists. Bank don't like me. Fact, they want to fire me already. I can tell."

Dan moved towards the flames in the fireplace.

"I'll help you get through this mess, Dan," I said. "Where's this cigarette pack now?"

"Right here," he said.

He took it out of his shirt pocket. It was inside a small ZipLoc plastic bag like the ones you buy in supermarkets.

"Your boy Marc here, he's the only one from work I ever had over here. I invited the others from work. No soap. Too busy. Marc and I been drinking buddies since he joined the bank. Kind I can trust. He asked me, put it in this bag. Now, I'm thinking, just get rid of it. No evidence."

"Dan, we can take it off your hands," I said.

With my eyes, I tried telling Marcus to stay quiet. Only one detective can negotiate. The other should cover all doorways, windows, relatives or friends.

"They'll frickin' FIRE me!"

"Dan, you're misreading things."

"No evidence!" he shouted. He threw the ZipLoc bag into the fire.

I lunged and reached for the pack and fell, eight feet from the fire. My walking stick dropped.

Marcus sprang up and thrust his hand into the fire.

"I'll get it!" Marcus shouted.

I smelled his shirt cuff burn. It smoked. He reached deeper. His skin burned now, smelling like a hotdog left on the griddle too long. Dan pushed Marcus. Marcus shoved Dan. Dan went down next to me on the floor. Marcus dug deeper in the fire.

The plastic bag came up smoking in Marcus' fingers.

"That hurts!" Marcus shouted.

"That's mine," Dan said.

He lunged for it.

I grabbed his arms at the elbows and slammed them towards the wall. Marcus went to the kitchen, putting water on his hand and still holding the bag.

"Leave it lay, Dan," I said. "Just tell the truth, partner, and it's all going to be easy. Nobody at the bank will ever know."

"Why not?"

"Let's take a ride to see a friend of mine. She'll explain it to you."

❧

Since they were both drunk, I had to drive down to the Post Office building and call Merilee Rush to open the Resident Agency.

Dozens of pickups and cars crowded into Shooters parking lot.

"Look at them damn drunk fools going into Shooters Bar," Marcus slurred.

"Tonight's their big anniversary party," Marcus went on.

She reminded me that she was off-duty and the Resident Agency was closed. I said that we had Dan in a receptive mood right now and that could change tomorrow. If Dan did not feel like going on the record, no judge would ever admit that cigarette pack as evidence.

Merilee showed up, wearing a blue jean jacket and pants ensemble that showed her strong frame.

She stared at both Marcus and Dan.

"I can't take a statement off a drunk," she said. "You should know that, Royster."

"Use initiative, Merilee," I said. "Take what you can now. Re-interview him tomorrow. It'll turn out okay. Then you can send the package to Washington."

"You're showing your age, Royster," she said. "We move faster than that now. No need to send it to the lab in Washington. We are modernized. And I did three years as a lab tech to qualify as an agent trainee. I'll dust the cigarette pack myself and see if we get any prints. And if they match. We've already got Crostwaite's complete sheet from the Sheriff."

She sighed and unlocked the door to the Resident Agency.

The office had a front reception desk, about a dozen cubbyholes and a large waiting area. Dan and Marcus and I sat in hard steel chairs under a big plaque with 1930s photos of agents slain on duty. Marcus kept putting cold water on his burned hand. The liquor dulled some of the pain.

Dan and Marcus argued football vigorously. I tuned out and tried dozing.

It did not work.

My cellphone hummed on 'vibrate.' I ignored it.

Merilee came out beaming.

"It's a match," she said. "Crostwaite's prints are on that plastic. He's got a tented arch that stands out nice and clear. In the morning, when Uncle Sam is paying me, I'll make application for an arrest warrant. Not bad for amateurs, guys."

"I'm going to be dying at work tomorrow," Dan said. "And I can't call in sick."

"I got some fantastic hangover remedy," Marcus said. "Dr. Klioffski's Upset Stomach Powders. But you've got to take it tonight. Let's stop at my place and I'll give you some. It might even help my goddamned hand. It's on your way home, anyway."

"Thank the Lord for friends like you," Dan said.

☙

We drove along Main Street and onto our driveway at Route 66 Arms.

"That a dog there in the driveway?" Marcus asked.

"Where?"

"Just at your headlights there," he said.

Something pale and white lay there. I braked and rolled out.

Bruised thighs shone. My gut went in and out like I was going to hurl. A shock of red hair covered the shoulders. I reached down and moved it. The head lolled sideways. A syrup of blood caked her face. Her green panties lay ripped and bloody. Cuts scored her arms.

My breath snaked back into me.

Caulk's words came back to me. I had gotten one of my Showbizzers killed.

The sour feeling corkscrewed through me. My head felt like it would burst. My arms ached to throw punches until they shattered someone.

I growled in rage. Words would not work. Then I tried again.

"That's Clytemnestra," I said. "She's dead. Someone raped her and broke her neck and got away."

CHAPTER 29

Showdown

"Look at the dirt there!" Marcus said.

The letters "CR" were scratched in the dirt.

"Clytemnestra's fingers are all dirty, man," Marcus said. "She must have been walking coming back home after barhopping, asking questions, flirting. You know Cly."

"We knew Cly."

"Then Crosswaite grabs her, tells her who he is and rapes her. Showing his power. She writes his name to tell us. He snaps her neck and runs."

Dan kept staring at the naked pale body and the red hair.

"She must have gotten something good," Marcus said. He was sobering up faster than Dan was. "Poor Cly. All broke up. Why didn't she tell us?"

Something chilled me. My feet moved just a millimeter or two. Then I dug out my cellphone.

"GODDAMNIT!" I shouted. "She did!"

At the house, Snowball barked.

Koy shouted at him.

"This is my fault" I said. "She was all wrong for this."

My eyes wetted.

"My phone has a text message from her," I shouted.

"I never goddamn checked it! Clytemnestra texted me. 'Midnight tonight at Shooters Bar. They stole cars to meet there. Partial plate is AHY. Crosswaite is driving a grey Toyota jeep. Dutch Door overheard him.' How could she get this?"

"Sex and bar-talk," Marcus snapped.

"What Clytemnestra did best. Her own art form. Tonight is Shooters Tenth anniversary party. Open bar from midnight to 12:30. They'll have hundreds of cheapskate drinkers there."

We stared at Clytemnestra's body.

"She paid for that message with her life, "

Marcus said. He cupped his hands and faced the Showbizzer house.

"Clytemnestra is dead! Everyone out here now!"

"I want to kill something!" Marcus snapped.

"Then come with me," I said. "Got the guts, you might get your chance."

"Call the cops."

"Call them and Crosswaite gets away," I said.

His head came up. Tears wet his cheeks.

We ran to the Roadmaster with Snowball barking. For once, I took the wheel. Tires screamed. My Showbizzers were shouting back and forth.

"Here take this." I handed Zygolt my cellphone. "Hit the number for FBI," My voice strained to sound calm. "Tell Merilee Rush everything we got. Convince her to call the Sheriff's inside line. Marcus, you call 911. Let's go, Showbizzers!"

☙

Main Street looked empty. Shooters Bar flashed in front of us. Cars, jeeps and pickups choked the parking lot. Locals hung outside. Their cigarettes glowed. White cowboy hats bobbed over gray smoke. Diesel fuel smell mixed with the smell of the desert. Western Swing music came from inside."

How do we find them?" Koy asked.

"The Showbizzer way," I said. "We bluff!"

I hit the horn. Our car fishtailed over asphalt.

"Run!" a beery-sounding woman shouted.

"He's crazy!" a Latino baritone hollered. We slewed into their parking lot. Locals scattered.

"Shoot that ranny!" Someone screamed. My head whipped around. I tried to see every car in the lot. No AHY plate showed.

"Max, we can't clear that bar in time!" Koy shouted.

"Oh, yes, I can!" I hollered.

"This is still Southern California!"

"What?" I aimed the Roadmaster at the first row of cars. My foot gunned the gas pedal. Fear brassed the taste in my mouth.

"The government can execute us all tomorrow," I said. "But, right now, we're in charge of Basta. It is butt-kicking night in Mad City."

We hit the first car. We crunched. Our car rocked back. I hit another car. Glass exploded. We skidded.

"This is getting easier!" I shouted. "I like this! I'm a hooligan!"

Three cars grouped at the curb of Main Street. They looked different from the others. Shapes slumped inside. One trunk opened and a man searched inside it.

"AHY!" Zygolt shouted.

"The license plate. And one is gray!"

Sirens sounded behind us. My hands twisted the wheel towards the three cars. We rocketed at them. Behind us, locals streamed out of Shooters. Some chased us.

"Bomb in Shooters!" Marcus screamed in his best Othello voice. "Clear out!"

A Basta police car roared up Main Street. The gray Jeep pulled away from the three cars. Shots flamed from inside the gray car.

"They're shooting at us!" Zygolt said.

Three Sheriff's cars screamed through the alley. More shots fired. A shotgun blasted. The gray Jeep fled.

"That's Crosswaite!" Koy shouted. "Don't let him get away!"

"Later," I said.

"He's running," Koy said.

"He's management," I said. "The supervisor."

Fear gave me tunnel vision. My Showbizzers were seeing more than I was. They were saving me. They were covering for me. The other car tried to flee. A cop car slammed into him. The fleeing car exploded. Flames shot upwards.

"Bombs," Zygolt said. "They were carrying bombs."

"For Crosswaite to destroy Basta," I said. "Like Quantrill in Kansas."

Cops and deputies jumped out of their cars. They blasted the last car with shotguns. Orange flames fire-balled through it. Two men lurched outside the car. They surrendered with hands high. One fell, blood on his legs.

"Look!" Marcus shouted. "Everybody's running out of Shooters. Bus boys, strippers, cooks. Max, how did you know how to do that?"

Windows blew out of Shooters. Smoke bloomed. Patrons screamed and ran. Glass shone. One wall of Shooters fell forward.

"Looks like everyone got out," Zygolt said.

"Max?"

"Now, we look for Crosswaite," I said.

"Come on, Max. How did you get them to leave?"

"If you want to get Southern Cal jokers out of a building," I said. "Just start hitting cars parked outside. At random. Every swinging mother's son will break their legs to run outside and protect their precious family automobile."

"Where are we going, Max?" Zygolt asked.

"Calico," I said.

"Crosswaite used to work there. It was his only refuge. His real home. I know there's a gate. But I bet he kept the keys. Government never changes locks. It costs too much."

"Why go there?"

"Because there is only a gate at the front. With a Jeep, food and water, he can hide out there forever or head out farther into the desert. A dozen roads can put him near Route 15 for Vegas or L.A."

❧

My speed scared me. The speedometer was cresting eighty as I flew towards the Freeway entrance.

"Did anyone ever tell you that you're a terrible driver?" Koy asked. She was crying.

"Three times a day. After meals."

"You trained us to plan ahead," Zygolt said. "If we see him, what then?"

"Marcus, you said you never hunted. Can you use a shotgun, Texas boy?"

"Not really."

"I can," Zygolt said. "I hunted ducks as a kid. Hand me that sucker. Clytemnestra was my friend."

"Don't shoot unless you have to," I said. "I taught you all self-defense law."

"This is no time for law."

"Yes, it is."

Highway 15 looked empty now. Our tires ate it up.

"Keep looking for a gray Toyota Jeep," I said. "Remember that Crosswaite has all the advantages. He saw us bust up his plot tonight. He could have some more gangsters with him, all armed. He knows the land around Calico and we don't."

"Clytemnestra must have asked too many questions," Koy said. She was crying. "She drew attention to herself."

"She always loved attention," Marcus said. "A true actress."

Zygolt took out the shotgun and racked the action.

"Max!" she shouted. "There's no shells! The shotgun is empty!"

My hands shook as I spun us over some sand.

"Well, Showbizzers," I said.

My voice half-giggled and half-wheezed from nerves.

"Like the Bible says, if you don't have the cards, then you can't deal them."

"Everybody check your pockets and the floor!" Marcus said. "We need those shells."

"Forget it," I said. "I left them in Koy's other purse. Then I had to unload this one. It's my fault."

Our Roadmaster took the turn-off to Calico. My knee ached. Something rubbery was burning under our hood.

My gut churned. Koy's tears did not help.

"Our only chance is surprise," I said. "This Roadmaster can't handle the desert. His Jeep can. If Crosswaite gets out there, he gets away."

We rocked along the dirt road. I cut our headlights.

The road forked to Calico.

"Marcus, hand me that crutch from the back seat," I said. "A pro always fights with any possible weapon. That's real strong wood. Time for some more crutch-fighting."

"Look up there!" Zygolt shouted.

A big Jeep was going through the open gates.

"Toyota!" Marcus shouted. "It's Crosswaite!"

❧

I was done talking.

I was done teaching.

Our car slammed into his Jeep's rear panel and spun him around. My head jolted back. Something else snapped in my shoulder.

"Awww!" Zygolt shouted.

Snowball barked.

Inside the Jeep, a pale face jolted from behind the steering wheel. Sideburns framed him.

It was Crosswaite.

He was bigger and wider than in the old photo. But it was him.

I drove the car right into his wheel well with all our speed. We crunched. Our front end jammed his Jeep.

It stopped.

Then the Jeep tried to power out. I kept him blocked in. His tires spun. Woodchips flew in his headlights. He reached to his right.

"Down!" I shouted.

Our windshield exploded.

"My eye!" Marcus shouted.

Crosswaite jumped out of his Jeep, a pump sawed-off shotgun in his hand. He started towards us.

Snowball yelped.

Crosswaite dodged backwards. He looked thick through the shoulders, from jail weightlifting. But he moved as fast as an athlete. I could not keep up with him. Snowball jumped out of the car. He ran at Crosswaite.

"Ohhhh!" Marcus shouted.

Crosswaite ran past the shack with the weapons and exhibits.

Snowball gained on him.

Crosswaite fired again. Buckshot whistled past us.

I tore out of the car and went after him. My foot kicked open the shack door. The inside was lit up by the Jeep headlights. My fingers grabbed a spear and an atl-atl from the wall.

Snowball was pounding closer. Koy and Marcus ran after him. Zygolt sprinted alongside. My heart hammered. My fingers slipped. I felt helpless.

In the half-light, I could see Crosswaite. He was running past the excavation pits. I tried jamming the atl-atl onto my wrist.

Snowball bounded closer to Crosswaite, barking. They were just ten feet apart.

My left knee screamed with pain. I had to stop.

The pain exploded. My knee folded under me. My head smacked the ground. It snapped back. The atl-atl and the spear dropped.

I could not stand.

Snowball barked.

Marcus held his eye, shouting.

"Koy!" I shouted. "I'm finished. Take the atl-atl. Put the end of the spear in the notch."

Koy bent down and grabbed the atl-atl. Her hands shook. She fitted the spear into the atl-atl.

She reached backwards with the atl-atl.

Crosswaite whipped around to face Snowball. The shotgun came up.

Koy flung the spear. It flew through the night. It wobbled and then straightened and arced and stuck in Crostwaite's gut.

The shotgun exploded. Snowball yelped. The shotgun dropped.

"Snowball!" Koy screamed.

She rushed past me and grabbed the spear stuck in Crosswaite. He was still standing. She shoved it in further and then back out. Crosswaite screamed. Crosswaite punched her. She kicked him between the legs and threw wild strikes at him.

"My dog!" she screamed. "Snowball!"

Marcus and Zygolt rushed up. Marcus hit Crosswaite with an elbow. Zygolt swung my shotgun butt against Crostwaite's head.

Crosswaite went down. Koy stabbed him in the leg. More blood gushed.

"You shot my dog!" Koy shouted. "I'm making a citizen's arrest! Or else kill you right here and now! Rape Clytemnestra and snap her neck! You should die, too!"

EPILOGUE

The deputies got to us first.

Then the county ambulance took Crosswaite handcuffed to his gurney with a big deputy watching him.

His ego surfaced. It forced him to talk. He bragged to the deputy about raping and killing Clytemnestra. Locals had pointed her out to him as a snitch asking too many questions. Koy's first spear strike had punctured his liver. But he would pull through and serve prison terms for robbery, rape and murder.

"I could have erased this town," he snarled. "Blow up Shooters, and every business on Main Street and all four gas stations in ten minutes flat. When these nuts stopped me, I had to leave my crew and run and try again next month."

Snowball limped. Most of the buckshot had missed him. Koy cried and petted him and ran her arms through his coat. A deputy put in a call for Animal Control to come and take Snowball for treatment.

A caravan of vans slewed into Calico as it was getting light. We watched.

The vans read KNZ-TV and KXY-TV on their sides. Jazzy-looking lady TV reporters scampered out and asked us a lot of fool questions.

I let Marcus do the talking. After all, he was the actor. He talked about us Showbizzers.

More paramedics came and worked on his eye cut by window glass and his burned hand.

Koy handed me my walking stick.

"I must be crazy," she said. "But, now, I want to stay with you."

My grin stretched. I breathed out.

"You've talked me into it," I said.

"But I still don't know about my tests," she said.

"Then we will wait and worry together," I said. "With Snowball at the foot of our bed as chaperone."

She kissed me. TV cameras filmed us.

"You still didn't pay me for the gasoline on our first date," she said.

Chris and Ted, the Calico bosses, showed up beaming and gracious in their Jeeps. They watched the deputies book the spear and the atl-atl as arrest evidence.

More cars got here. Merilee Combs, looking official in her blue windbreaker with "FBI Special Agent" in butter colors across the back, got out of her car.

"They are already broadcasting your story on the radio, Royster," she said. "But it won't work. Show people can't police. They'll be just vigilantes."

I grinned.

Then helicopter noise buzz-sawed overhead.

The helicopter banked, turned on the landing lights and set down. A gold star on the green fuselage read "San Risa Sheriff's Department."

The Sheriff strode out, holding down his cowboy hat against the rotor blast.

The TV crews raced to him. Their lights showed his good-looking face with the weathered skin and wise eyes.

Another paramedic, an aging hippie with a white ponytail, looked at my left knee's scar, whistled and said an interesting gerund.

The Sheriff ground out his interview with the right pauses and smiles, recalling the first names of the reporters.

"Sure, I knew all about the Showbizzers," he said. "It is a fascinating concept, blending the creativity of the arts with the needs of law enforcement."

"I wish that I had said that," I said to Koy.

She rested her head on my shoulder. Even that hurt my knee.

"Maybe you should talk about the actress Clytemnestra," Marcus said in his deep delivery voice. "She was a gifted actress who gave her life to see this concept work."

"Now she'll be famous," Zygolt said. "Just like she wanted."

"Under proper supervision and training, these Showbizz-ers should be able to do anything," the Sheriff said.

"I always said so," I said.

"Showbizzers, break a leg and crush crime!" Zygolt shouted.

The Showbizzers cheered.

Some of the cameras picked up my wisecrack. The Sher-iff's smile faltered but it hung on.

"They can go places, infiltrate where deputies cannot and approach all kinds of people," he said.

"Like real, humane, sensitive cops should be able to do," I said.

He shot me a look to shut me up.

The Showbizzers surrounded and hugged whatever parts of me that they could reach. Dirt showed on our faces and clothes. My body groaned with the pain. Koy kissed me.

"In fact, I've got four Reserve Deputies stars in my pocket right now," he said. "I can swear them in right now and have them join our next Reserve Academy class. Once gradu-ated, they will have full police powers."

"My man," my hippie paramedic said. "You have tore up your new knee operation to a fare-thee-well. Our surgeon is going to have to re-operate to repair you. I'd say three months on crutches for you. Maybe more."

"Keep your Reserve Deputy stars, Sheriff," I said as the cameras filmed me. "Me and my Showbizzers have to stay clear of all government in order to work our next case."

Special thanks once again to:

To Detective-Investigators Mark Baldessare and Fareed "Fred" Ghussin and all the other cops and federal agents who taught me so much about hunting our real-life serial killers.

To the *Spy, the Movie* team – Jim MacPherson, Alex Klymko, Charles Messina and all the rest of the gang for a grand adventure in screenwriting.

To Nad Wolinska for her as always inventive cover illustration and Richard Amari for his equally inventive cover design.

To my editor, Lynwood Shiva Sawyer, for his support and encouragement over the years

And my thanks to that wonderful woman, companion and friend from Guangzhou, China, who shares my adventures and my life.

The next Max Royster story is coming soon!

I, Max Royster, NYPD cop cashiered "for mental disease or defect", resume the only activity that still brings me joy, ballroom dancing.

And I fall in love.

My new flame lives in Flatbush, Brooklyn, a neighborhood that used to be Brooklyn's jewel. The Brooklyn Dodgers and Jackie Robinson had played ball there.

Back then, nobody in Flatbush locked their doors.

But now, fifty years later, street crime plagues Flatbush.

Robberies and shootings increase. Eventually, someone murders a black community activist.

I get a chance to boss a private security outfit.

Somehow, I think I can inspire my guards.

Using my cop tricks, I can change them from unhappy minimum wage-earners to passionate, hardworking crime fighters.

Do you know how many guards work in security?

Think of the potential. Tracking suspects, I penetrate a White Supremacist gang. They may have killed the activist.

I keep digging. My lover and her friends want the area to improve. The Flatbush image will soften. That way, they can flip their homes for a profit and move away.

So I call her friends "Flippers," a term that does not amuse them. At the same time, I must control my guards, who want to bully everyone.

Come walk with me on that razor's edge between brutality and staying alive as my Flippers do their best at *Softening Flatbush*.

If you enjoyed reading *Can Showbizzers Crush Crime?*, you'll definitely like Frank Hickey's other Max Royster novels:.

Brownstone Kidnap Crackup

When Max witnesses a debutante's kidnapping, he becomes the FBI's prime suspect. Or is he actually their salvation?

It's Christmas in Manhattan.

A blizzard whips the city.

The Beautiful People, in the elite Upper East Side, celebrate in their brownstones.

Until a kidnapper seizes a beautiful young debutante.

Max Royster, fired from the NYPD for mental illness, fights the kidnapper but loses.

The kidnapper flees. Stripped of gun, shield and power, Max has only his wits to save the victim.

The FBI treats Max like a suspect and tramples roughshod on his rights.

During this long sleepless night, an unknown FBI agent cracks up. Over the radio, he quotes J. Edgar Hoover and plants false clues.

To solve the case, Max must smash through the facade and mysteries of millionaires in their snug brownstones.

Exotic women tempt him to give up.

The blizzard worsens.

As the winds howl and snowdrifts deepen, Max risks his life and his freedom in a desperate bid to save the victim.

Once again, Max Royster is back on the street in *Brownstone Kidnap Crackup*.

Funny Bunny Hunts the Horn Bug

To catch a sex killer targeting Upper East Side beauties, misfit NYPD cop Max Royster goes undercover....as an NYPD cop!

The Upper East Side of Manhattan is one of the richest neighborhoods in the world.

But Max Royster, a maverick, outspoken and erudite NYPD foot cop, who grew up working-class in this tony area, calls it "the Playpen." Money protects the bluebloods in this area like the bars on an infant's playpen.

Late one night, patrolling wealthy brownstones, he sees a burglar attacking a rich actress. Max chases him. They fight but the burglar escapes.

The burglar is a sexual predator, known in cop-speak as a "Horn Bug."

For losing the suspect, Max's captain deems Max "a Funny Bunny," too unstable for police work. He strips Max of his gun and badge, then orders Max into Bellevue Hospital for observation and maybe for the rest of his life.

Without any tools or support, Max ten days to stop this Horn Bug.

The Gypsy Twist

".... Max looked carefully at the dead boy, reminding himself that most murder victims looked very young and surprised when their bodies were found, as if life had suddenly rushed up and taken them unawares ...."

Max Royster's hunt for a sadistic serial killer takes a startling turn when he realizes that not all predators are born alike.